"Michelle! Good To See You!"

Smiling with delight, Steve Saraceni rose from his chair and offered her his outstretched hand.

How did he do it? Michelle Carey wondered. His smile looked so genuine. He even managed to make his dark eyes shine with warmth and sincerity. He was the most sophisticated, handsome man she'd ever met. She'd never stood a chance.

Michelle did not offer her hand in return, forcing Steve to drop his to his side.

"What brings you here today?" he asked.

"I don't want to take up any more of your valuable time than is absolutely necessary," Michelle said tautly. "I—I'm only here because I thought you have a—" She paused and gulped. "You have a moral right to know."

She raised her head, and her china-blue eyes met his cool dark ones. "I'm pregnant."

Dear Reader,

Happy 1992, and welcome to Silhouette Desire! For those of you who are new readers, I must say I think you're starting the year off right—with wonderful romance. If you're a regular Desire fan, you already know what delicious stories are in store for you... this month *and* this year. I wish I could tell you the exciting things planned for you in 1992, but that would be giving all of my secrets away. But I will admit that it's going to be a great year.

As for January, what better way to kick off a new year of *Man of the Month* stories than with a sensuous, satisfying love story from Ann Major, *A Knight in Tarnished Armor*. And don't miss any of 1992's *Man of the Month* books, including stories written by Diana Palmer, Annette Broadrick, Dixie Browning, Sherryl Woods and Laura Leone—and that's just half of my lineup!

This month is completed with books by Barbara Boswell, Beverly Barton, Cathryn Clare, Jean Barrett and Toni Collins. They're all terrific; don't miss a single one.

And remember, don't hesitate to write and tell me what you think of the books. I'm always glad to receive reader feedback.

So go wild with Desire... until next month,

Lucia Macro
Senior Editor

BARBARA BOSWELL
LICENSE TO LOVE

SILHOUETTE *Desire*®

Published by Silhouette Books New York

America's Publisher of Contemporary Romance

SILHOUETTE BOOKS
300 East 42nd St., New York, N.Y. 10017

LICENSE TO LOVE

ISBN: 0-373-05685-0

First Silhouette Books printing January 1992

Printed in the U.S.A.

Books by Barbara Boswell

Silhouette Desire

Rule Breaker #558
Another Whirlwind Courtship #583
The Bridal Price #609
The Baby Track #651
License To Love #685

BARBARA BOSWELL

loves writing about families. "I guess family has been a big influence on my writing," she says. "I particularly enjoy writing about how my characters' family relationships affect them."

When Barbara isn't writing and reading, she's spending time with her *own* family—her husband, three daughters and three cats, whom she concedes are the true bosses of their home! She has lived in Europe, but now makes her home in Pennsylvania. She collects miniatures and holiday ornaments, tries to avoid exercise and has somehow found the time to write over twenty category romances.

Prologue

July 2

"Michelle! Good to see you!" Smiling with apparent delight, Steve Saraceni rose from his desk chair. "And how's everything over at Senator Dineen's office?"

His affable greeting was so unexpected that it had the effect of stopping Michelle Carey dead in her tracks. So that was the way he was going to play it? As if they were two longtime colleagues, veterans of the Pennsylvania political scene, amiably discussing the *weather!* As if the last time they had seen each other, they hadn't parted in a wild, passionate lover's quarrel.

How did he do it? Michelle wondered bleakly. His smile looked so genuine. He even managed to make his dark eyes shine with warmth and sincerity. Whatever his feelings, that smooth, smiling mask of his never slipped. At least not in public. In their private times together, she'd seen the man behind the mask. She'd fallen in love with him. But they were alone now and she was being subjected to the public, impenetrable Steve. Pain ripped through her.

Steve walked around his desk and crossed the office, extending his hand to her for a friendly shake. The image he projected appealed to both men and women alike. Approachable, eminently likable, earnest and honest. Lobbyists—and he was a lobbyist consultant representing a number of clients—were sometimes viewed as aggressive, slick and cool, but Steve Saraceni never came across that way. He had never met anyone he couldn't eventually charm into liking him. In the land mine field of politics Steve Saraceni was without enemies, truly an awesome feat and a telling tribute to his persuasive skills.

He was the most sophisticated, self-confident man Michelle had ever met, a man who wielded his appeal and charm with the precision of a lethal weapon. She hadn't stood a chance, she acknowledged miserably. How naive she'd been to believe otherwise.

Michelle did not offer her hand in return, forcing Steve to drop his to his side. It was a small but definite victory because there was nothing he hated more than looking foolish. He rarely, if ever, did. Steve Saraceni always managed to appear in the right place at the right time with the right people . . . doing just the right thing—or what appeared to be the right thing.

Which brought her to the point of her visit. Michelle's mouth was suddenly dry. Was she doing the right thing by coming here and telling him? She'd spent hours debating the issue with herself, wildly vacillating from one position to the other. Her heart slammed against her ribs, beating so hard and so fast, she was surprised it wasn't externally visible.

"What brings you here today, Michelle?" Steve asked. His deep voice was pleasant but impersonal.

It was the same tone he would use to ask a passerby on the street for the correct time. That he would use it with her hurt terribly because there was a time when his voice had been husky and intimate and laced with affection. Michelle wondered if there was another woman in his life being treated to those same smoky, sexy tones of his. Knowing Steve's reputation, there probably was.

Her heart clenched as a spasm of pain shot through her. But with the pain came another emotion superceding it. Fury.

Michelle fought to suppress it. She couldn't have an emotional outburst, she must stay as cool and calm as he. If that were possible, she thought grimly. Steve Saraceni personified cool.

"I don't want to take up any more of your valuable time than is absolutely necessary," Michelle said tautly. "I—I'm only here because I thought you have a—" she paused and gulped. Both her nerve and her resolve were fading fast. If she didn't tell him right now, she never would. "You have a moral right to know." She raised her head and her wide-set china blue eyes met his cool dark ones. "I'm pregnant."

Her words hit him with the force and power of a bullet right between the eyes. Steve jerked backward and stumbled against his desk. He leaned against it, grateful for something solid to hold on to, because the room seemed to be spinning around at whirlwind velocity. He opened his mouth to speak, but no words came out.

It was the first time in his life that the golden gift of speech failed him. His breathing and swallowing abilities seemed to be out of order, too. His mouth was so dry he felt as if he were gagged with a yard of cotton wool. When he tried to inhale, nothing happened.

"Wh-what?" Steve finally managed to ask. He sounded winded, as if he'd been socked in the solar plexus.

He felt that way, too. It was exactly the same way he'd felt back in college. He'd been a wide receiver for Penn State, and the opposing team's two hundred-ten-pound defensive lineman had smashed into him while he was running toward the end zone, clutching the football. Steve had de-

cided at that moment that there had to be an easier way than
a football career to acquire the wealth and status he had always longed for. He quit the team, dropped his dreams for
a pro career and turned his energies to a future in politics.
It seemed a suitable, pain-free alternative and when he'd
learned about the influential, freewheeling, lucrative life of
legislative lobbyists, he'd known that was the career he'd
been born for.

He was an unqualified success at it. There were chal-
lenges, but none he couldn't handle. And then he'd met
Michelle Carey, assistant administrative aide to state senator Edward Dineen. A challenge? Perhaps. But his confidence had never flagged. He could handle her.

Or so he'd thought. Steve managed to focus his eyes on
Michelle, who stood before him, her face pale and drawn.
Odd that someone her size had managed to level him as ef-
fectively as that helmeted behemoth from the University of
Miami, he thought numbly.

She was only average height, about five feet four inches,
although her high-heeled pumps gave her the illusion of
tallness. She was slightly built, her frame small-boned, her
figure slender. Slender but curvy...in all the right places. His
eyes swept reflexively over her. She was wearing a no-
nonsense blue suit and cream-colored blouse buttoned to the
neck, but instead of negating her shapeliness, the modestly
proper outfit somehow enhanced it.

Or maybe it was his imagination at work instead, remembering the fullness of her breasts, the silky skin of her
abdomen, the womanly curves of her hips. Steve felt a band
of heat tighten in his groin. Michelle was blond and lovely,
with ivory skin, high cheekbones and a soft wide mouth that
beckoned and tempted. He'd been sexually attracted to her
from the first time they'd met, though she had been careful
to maintain an all-business, hands-off demeanor.

He'd been challenged, then intrigued. There had never
been a woman that Steve Saraceni wanted but couldn't get.

But then, Michelle Carey wasn't supposed to be one of his women; she was business. He knew it was dangerous to combine the two, but he'd thought he could handle it.

Suddenly the air seemed very thin. When he finally breathed, it came out like more of a gasp. "How?" he choked.

Michelle stared at the thick, wine-colored carpet on the floor. "You know how," she whispered. Her face felt hot and she was beginning to perspire.

"But—but we've been careful!" Steve protested. This isn't happening, his mind screamed. It isn't possible! Unplanned, unwanted, unwed pregnancies happened to foolish teenagers, not to a successful thirty-four-year-old lobbyist whose income came close to matching his ego.

Michelle bit her lip, which was beginning to quiver. "Obviously we weren't careful enough."

Obviously not. Steve thought back to a certain night when he'd been feeling cocky and reckless and on top of the world. Throwing away caution had been easy. He was a risk-taker by nature and that particular risk had seemed negligible in comparison to his burning desire. After all, he was invulnerable to consequences!

Except, it seemed, to this tiny, unseen one concealed inside Michelle's still-flat belly. Steve went hot, then cold. Inside his head, he heard his sister Jamie's voice clear as a bell. "Heaven help you, when you finally fall," Jamie had said, her voice ominous, her dark eyes flashing disapproval. He had laughed at her. Upright, starchy Jamie; she was always lecturing him about his high-flying life. What did she know?

Steve grimaced. "Michelle, are you sure?" Denial surged through him. There was always the chance that she was mistaken. Wasn't there?

"Of course I'm sure," Michelle said coldly. "Do you really think I'd come here and—and put myself through this if I weren't?"

"I don't know, would you? After the—uh, disagreement—we had, you might be seeking revenge. And this would certainly be an effective—"

"Let's drop the sugar-coated doublespeak, Steve. What we had was a fight not a disagreement. And if I was looking for revenge, which I'm not, it wouldn't involve humiliating myself like this, trust me."

"You find me capable of trust?" he asked, sarcasm sharpening his tone. "That's surprising, considering that the last time we were together you called me a back-stabbing double-crosser."

"What did you expect?" she cried. "You are one!"

Steve shifted uncomfortably. He didn't like feeling in the wrong, he much preferred to think well of himself. It was time to put a new spin on the situation. He was very good at that.

"Michelle, you simply don't understand the dynamics of—" He paused after one glance at the closed, shuttered look on her face. "Oh, why bother to even try to explain? You don't want to understand, you prefer to see me as an unscrupulous cad who—"

"I didn't come here to argue," Michelle cut in. She was beginning to feel dangerously light-headed. Blindly, she crossed the office and sank down onto the leather sofa located perpendicular to the desk. She rested her elbows on her knees and slowly lowered her head, bracing her forehead with her hands. Her dark blond hair tumbled around her shoulders in tousled disarray.

Steve panicked. His experience with pregnant women was nil. "Michelle, are you all right?" Before racing to her side, he punched the button of his intercom. "Saran, bring some water! Quick!"

Moments later his young cousin Saran, who worked as his receptionist when the spirit moved her, appeared with a glass of water.

He snatched the glass and held it to Michelle's lips. "Here, drink this," he said hoarsely.

Michelle pushed it away. "I don't want it," she whispered. She sat pale and still in the chair, a fine sheen of perspiration covering her face.

Steve stood up and glanced wildly around the office. He noticed his cousin eyeing Michelle curiously. Saran could be a conniving little eavesdropper, he knew. It was imperative to get her out of the office. "Saran, I can manage now. Why don't you run along to lunch?"

Those were always welcome words to Saran. She quickly departed, calling an enthusiastic goodbye.

Michelle and Steve were alone in the office once again. She cast a covert glance at him. He bore no resemblance to the cool smooth operator who glided through life with his aura of invincible finesse. Michelle was horrified that she wanted to console him, to restore his jaunty male confidence. To put her arms around him and—

She gave her head a shake, as if to expel such traitorous thoughts. *She had to get out of here!* Because she had been so in love with him, he was a living, breathing danger zone. Not that she was still in love with him, Michelle hastened to reassure herself. Learning that he'd used her and lied to her had effectively expunged her love for him, she was certain of that. Still, old habits died hard and it was in her best interests to get away from him as quickly as possible.

Michelle stood up and was relieved that she no longer felt dizzy. The feeling of faintness had passed. "I shouldn't have come. It was a mistake. I shouldn't have told you."

"Of course you should have told me," snapped Steve. "Since you're accusing me of fatherhood, I at least deserve to know about it."

She bristled at his choice of words. "I wasn't accusing you, I was informing you. And I'm sorry that I did. You can forget all about it, Steve. I don't want or need anything from you." She started toward the door.

He caught her arm, restraining her. "What are you going to do?"

"That is none of your business."

"The hell it isn't! You come in here and announce that you're pregnant and then tell me to forget about it? I don't think so, Michelle."

She jerked her arm free. "Just tell yourself that you aren't responsible. Tell yourself that I'm easy; there could be any number of men who might be the father; you're an innocent man who's been wrongly accused."

"Shut up!"

His vehemence surprised them both. A tense silence filled the room. Going ballistic would only exacerbate matters, Steve admonished himself. The secret to skillful negotiating was to keep cool, stay calm. He cleared his throat. He even managed a small smile, though it was far removed from the high-voltage grins he usually flashed. "Nothing is ever accomplished in the heat of anger," he said in measured, conciliatory tones. "Let's sit down and we'll discuss—"

"That's more like the Steve Saraceni I know," Michelle cut in caustically. "Right down to the trust-me-I'm-on-your-side smile."

His smile faded abruptly. "That's not fair, Michelle. I'm trying to..."

"...Do damage control while you assess your options?"

"...Keep steady and think clearly," Steve corrected with a frown of disapproval.

"Am I supposed to congratulate you on your efforts? I probably am. You're used to congratulations, you're used to doing what you want and getting what you want. You're not only used to it, you expect it!"

Her voice had risen and she was on the verge of tears. Once again, a wave of panic assailed him. The prospect of a hysterical pregnant woman was as unnerving as a sick one. "Michelle, I'm doing my best to—"

"Yes, you always do your best. You're infallible, a winner."

A fulsome compliment he had heard before, but she'd turned it around and made him sound odious. Steve scowled. "Michelle, I'm a patient man but you aren't making this easy for either of us."

No, she wasn't, Michelle silently agreed. She didn't know why. After all, he hadn't done any of the things she had envisioned in her worst-case-scenario nightmares. He hadn't denied paternity, he hadn't announced that it was her problem, not his. He hadn't thrown her out of the office, threatening her reputation and her livelihood.

He hadn't taken her in his arms and told her he loved her, either. He hadn't kissed her, whispering that he'd been in agony since their breakup, that he'd been dreaming of a reconciliation and her appearance in his office was an answer to his prayers. He hadn't said he was thrilled that the woman he loved was carrying his child and from now on they were all going to live happily together.

What a fool she was! Unwelcome tears filled Michelle's eyes. Twenty-five years old, unmarried and pregnant by a man who didn't love her, a man who enthusiastically extolled the pleasures of bachelorhood and made no secret of his intention to remain single.

And if she didn't get away from him quickly, she was going to be crying—like a baby. She flinched at the imagery.

"I apologize for failing to appreciate your efforts to be patient and keep steady and think clearly," Michelle said, striving to hide her teary weakness behind a show of bravado. "How rude of me to be ungrateful when you've been such a champ. Now, if you'll excuse me, I have a one o'clock meeting with Senator Dineen. I'm sure you must have a meeting yourself."

She promptly rushed from the office.

Her abrupt departure caught Steve off guard. She was out of the suite of offices and striding down the corridor before he caught up with her. He followed her to the elevator, amidst the busy flow of lunch-hour traffic.

Michelle pressed the call button, then impatiently pressed it again.

"All right, go to your meeting," Steve said, keeping his voice low and out of earshot of the four others who'd joined them at the elevator. "We'll talk later. I'll come over tonight and—"

"Save yourself the trip," she whispered. "I won't be home."

The elevator arrived and its passengers filed out. "Where will you be?" Steve demanded. Impulsively he caught her wrist and tugged her toward him.

Michelle tugged back. Though he kept hold of her, her outstretched arm kept a distance between them. "I'm going to my stepsister's for the Fourth of July weekend, not that it's any concern of yours."

He ignored the gibe. "But it's only Wednesday. Why are you leaving tonight? Are you taking tomorrow off? Which sister are you visiting?"

"You sound like a prosecutor grilling a witness on the stand. A definite departure from your usual smooth way of weasling information." Michelle glanced pointedly at his hand on her wrist. The elevator was beginning to load. She took a step toward it.

His fingers tightened, halting her. Reflexively her eyes flew to his face. A mistake on her part, Michelle conceded as his gaze met and held hers. His velvety dark brown eyes were compelling and intense. Those soul-piercing stares of his had always had a mesmerizing effect on her. He had such power over her, Michelle acknowledged miserably. The fact that she had freely given him that power was little consolation.

"Let me go, Steve," she said breathlessly. "We—we'll talk later."

"Tonight." It was a statement, not a request.

Michelle glanced at the passengers in the elevator who were beginning to stare at her. They looked impatient, ready to leave her behind if she didn't board.

"All right. Tonight," she agreed quickly.

"We'll have dinner. I'll be over shortly before six." He released her wrist.

Michelle rushed into the elevator, the doors snapped shut, and the car descended.

Steve was at the door of her apartment at approximately 5:43 p.m. In one hand he clutched a bouquet of carnations, daisies and ferns, which he had purchased from a street vendor. Was it appropriate to bring flowers to the woman who claimed to be carrying his child? He usually had an instinctive feel about how to proceed in any given situation, but the etiquette for this one totally eluded him.

He was very aware of his pounding heart and churning stomach, physical symptoms of anxiety that he found extremely unpleasant. He wasn't used to them; he'd never been the nervous type. Not even as an adolescent had he experienced the palm-sweating, throat-clogging anxiety of his peers.

But he was suffering it now, with a vengeance.

He knocked at the door. There was no response. He knocked again and then pressed the buzzer. Still no sounds from within. Steve glanced at his Rolex watch, one of his most treasured possessions, a status symbol that thrilled him every time he looked at it. He'd told Michelle shortly before six. Perhaps she hadn't returned from her office yet. She certainly wouldn't expect him to be early.

Eventually he tired of waiting at her door and returned to his car, a sleek black Jaguar, another treasured possession, another status symbol that thrilled him every time he drove it. He'd illegally parked it directly in front of the building and he sat behind the wheel, watching and waiting for Michelle to arrive.

She didn't. At six-thirty, he marched back up to her apartment and pounded on the door. Nothing. Frustrated, muttering a curse, he leaned on the buzzer. It sounded, nonstop. He pounded on the door with his other hand. He knew he was making a terrible racket and didn't care. He willed the door to open.

It didn't, but the door across the hall did, and a middle-aged woman appeared, looking annoyed. "There's nobody home there," the woman said. "She's gone for the long holiday weekend."

"Gone?" Steve was flabbergasted. "But we were supposed to have dinner!"

The woman shrugged. "Looks like you've been stood up." The door closed.

Stood up! Steve was staggered. It was unthinkable, an alien concept. Michelle had stood him up.

He was still in shock as he drove himself and his cousin Saran back to the Saraceni family home in the small working-class town of Merlton, New Jersey, for his parents' annual Fourth of July barbecue.

It was an event he would've preferred to skip, particularly now, but he had learned over the years that it was easier if he was present at family holiday affairs. His absence guaranteed worried and/or scolding phone calls from each and every family member, not to mention the possibility of any one of them turning up on his doorstep "just to make sure he was all right."

But it was not his loving family—whose possessive devotion he viewed as suffocating and smothering—that dominated his thoughts on that dismal drive to New Jersey. Images of Michelle kept tumbling through his mind, kaleidoscope fashion: Michelle loving him, and now, hating him.

He thought back to the first time he had seen her, six months ago. He'd met her shortly afterward. How had it come to this? Steve wondered bleakly....

In the suburban Washington, D.C. home of her stepsister Courtney Tremaine, Michelle was equally preoccupied with memories of Steve. While she went through the motions of talking and laughing with Courtney and her husband Connor, of oohing and ahhing over the cuteness of their three-month-old adopted daughter Sarah, her mind replayed every scene with Steve from the moment they'd met until their most recent encounter—that tense, unhappy confrontation in his office. Her heart was truly broken. She should have known it would come to this....

One

January, six months earlier

"A chain letter!" Michelle scowled at the letter she'd just opened, then crumpled it up and tossed it into the trashcan alongside her desk.

"You're not going to, uh, pass it along to anybody?" asked Brendan O'Neal. He was a part-time law student who worked as an intern in Senator Dineen's office and was unofficially Michelle's assistant.

"I wouldn't waste the time. I wouldn't foist one of those idiotic letters on anybody." She grinned. "Not even on Joe McClusky and his staff."

Senator Joe McClusky was one of Senator Ed Dineen's arch rivals in the Pennsylvania state senate. As Senator Dineen's assistant administrative aide, Michelle was fiercely loyal to her boss and therefore inimical toward the McClusky forces.

"It's supposed to be bad luck not to pass along a chain letter." Brendan retrieved the discarded paper from the trash, smoothed out the wrinkles and read it. "According to this, there are dire consequences for not sending this letter to somebody else. Listen to what happened to the ones who didn't—one guy had a winning lottery ticket for a ten-million-dollar jackpot and then lost the ticket, another guy was killed in a plane crash, a woman lost her home and all her possessions in a mysterious flash fire." He glanced at Michelle. "Are you sure you want to mess with this? You could send it to me and beat the curse. Then *I'll* pass it on to McClusky."

Michelle laughed. "You and your Irish mysticism!" She snatched the letter from him and threw it back into the trashcan. "I won't be intimidated by those bogus threats. Chain letters like these are illegal anyway."

"Okay, okay. But may I suggest not buying a lottery ticket or an airplane ticket or lighting a match until the alleged curse wears off. Whenever that is."

She glared at him in mock severity. "Brendan, go to lunch."

He gave an equally mock salute. "Yes, ma'am."

Brendan had been gone less than ten minutes when the door to her office opened again. Michelle suppressed a sigh. This was at least the fifth or sixth interruption of the morning, not including the ubiquitous phone calls. She had a small mountain of reading material on her desk pertaining to the new federal demands concerning hazardous waste sites and exactly two days to get through it before the committee meeting. At this rate she would be reading well into the night to make the deadline.

"I hope you'll forgive me for barging in like this."

The voice was deep, smooth, and contained a perfect blend of apology and humor. Michelle glanced up at once. Standing in the doorway was a man whose looks exceeded the clichéd tall, dark and handsome stereotype. She stared at him a moment too long, but she couldn't help herself. He was that gorgeous.

He was about six feet tall and his gray suit appeared custom-tailored for his superb, muscular frame. But it was his face that riveted Michelle. He had been blessed with a marvelous combination of bone structure and coloring and the results were breathtaking. Literally. Michelle had to remind herself to exhale as she gazed at his impossibly sensual mouth, which was drawn into the most beguiling, appealing smile she had ever seen. His eyes were a dark velvety brown in color and glowed with an alert intelligence and inviting warmth that beckoned and compelled.

Charisma. The word immediately came to mind. He'd been abundantly gifted with that elusive but unmistakable quality along with his stunning looks.

He walked toward her, smiling that smile, exuding confidence, virile magnetism and an irresistible sexual allure. "I'm Steve Saraceni." He held out his hand to her. "And I know you're Michelle Carey, Senator Dineen's assistant administrative aide and his acting liaison to the committee studying the hazardous waste elimination bill."

Automatically she gave him her hand. His fingers closed around hers in a firm shake. Michelle's heart began to pound and she felt her skin flush. If his looks packed a potent wallop, the effects of his touch probably registered on the Richter scale. When she found herself checking his left hand for a wedding band—he wasn't wearing one—she knew it was time to end this mind-bending handshake.

Michelle took a bolstering step backward, embarrassed by her unexpected, uncharacteristic response to the man. She was a mature professional woman, not a giddy schoolgirl, she reminded herself sternly.

It was time to regain control of the situation... and of herself! "Mr. Saraceni," she began.

"Call me Steve, everybody does."

Before she could reply, he whipped out his business card and pressed it into her hand. She glanced at it. Legislative Engineers Limited was printed in bold black print with the names Steven Saraceni, Patrick Lassiter and Gregory Arthur in smaller letters underneath.

Michelle arched her brows. "Legislative Engineers?"

"I know, I know. Sounds pretentious, doesn't it? Greg, one of my partners, came up with it. He thought it had more panache than Lobbyists for Hire, which is what we actually are."

"You're a lobbyist," Michelle repeated. "Of course. I should have known."

"Uh-oh. I hope that doesn't mean, 'Of course, a slick, fast-talking, back-slapping arm-twister.'" Steve's smile was wry, his tone self-deprecating. "I know that's a common perception of lobbyists but I've tried to go against the ingrained stereotype. I don't slap backs and I don't twist arms, Michelle. I simply do the job I've been hired to do—that is, to present my clients' views to the legislators."

He was serious, earnest and sincere. Michelle felt a pang of guilt for the lobbyist-bashing she and other staffers periodically indulged in. "I just meant that I should've known a legislative engineer is another term for lobbyist," she said quickly. "I've heard it before, but not very often."

"Probably the same semantics genius who invented domestic engineer for housewife came up with legislative engineer for lobbyist." Steve smiled ingenuously. "Anyway, I know how busy you must be and I won't take up any more of your time. I just wanted to introduce myself to you and invite you and the rest of the committee studying the bill on hazardous waste elimination to lunch."

His smile broadened and there was humor in his warm dark eyes. "Hmm, that didn't come out very well—mentioning lunch and hazardous waste in the same breath. Can I try it again? I'll try to come up with something a shade more, er, appetizing."

His good humor was infectious. Michelle couldn't help but smile back. But she did remember her position and his, and asked, "What is your interest in the bill?"

"My client is Allied Medical Technologies, Incorporated. They build incinerators that burn medical waste from hospitals, doctors' offices and labs. They would like to be awarded the contract to build incinerators on the sites selected by the state, so they're very interested in this bill Senator Dineen is sponsoring. As AMT's lobbyist, I'd like to meet the committee members and present pertinent information to them before the bill is voted out of committee and sent to the floor."

"I see," said Michelle. And she did. If his efforts were successful to his client's cause, he would earn a substantial bonus in addition to the annual retainer paid by the company. The bonus sum grew with each degree of success achieved, beginning with getting a bill introduced, escalating to getting it through a committee and finally paying off big if the bill passed the state House and Senate.

Most of the lobbyists in Harrisburg were lawyers, trade association representatives or public relations consultants, full-time employees of corporations, labor unions or special interest groups. Steve and his partners were independent "hired guns" who represented dozens of different clients, firms that didn't want a full-time lobbyist, only a representative on certain, specific issues.

"I understand the committee will be meeting again next week," Steve continued. "May I take all of you to lunch the day before? If that's not okay for everyone, we'll reschedule at your convenience, of course. I'm nothing if not accommodating." His grin playfully mocked himself and the entire system.

He was upfront about his intentions and the procedure to be followed. Michelle thought he was a refreshing change from the smarmy types who tried to pretend that lobbyist/legislative socializing was something more than purely business. The difference between business associates and personal friends had always been quite clear to her.

She reminded herself of that fact now, when she found herself smiling at Steve in a certain way—the way a woman would smile at a man she was attracted to, with her head demurely tilted, her eyelashes lowered, her lips slightly parted. Quickly, Michelle tried to rearrange her face into the kind of professional smile reserved for lobbyists like Don Exner, a fifty-one-year-old, five foot eight, two hundred pound, married father of four.

Flushing, she thought she saw a knowing gleam in Steve's eyes, as if he knew exactly the effect he was having upon her. He probably did, Michelle decided grimly. A man with his looks had to be accustomed to women swooning over him, even throwing themselves at him. Not that she'd done either! Nor would she.

"I'll relay your invitation to lunch to the committee and get back to you," she said briskly. Yes, that was better. It was exactly the way she sounded when replying to Don Exner or any other lobbyist.

"Thank you, Michelle. I'll look forward to hearing from you."

It was a generic statement somehow made to sound promisingly intimate by his whiskey-smooth tones. His departing smile left her weak-kneed. Michelle ran her hand over her neatly French-braided blond hair and sought to regain her equilibrium from the sensual onslaught. It was as if Cupid had started shooting ballistic missiles instead of arrows.

Shortly after his departure, Claire Collins and Leigh Wilson, two other Dineen staffers, rushed into Michelle's office.

"Who was that guy? I couldn't believe my eyes!" exclaimed Leigh. "I looked up and there he was—a Greek god come to life!"

"She was speechless, all right," seconded Claire. "Leigh looked at him, opened her mouth and not a single word came out.'' She did a comic imitation of Leigh, staring glassy-eyed and slack-jawed.

"Don't tell me you weren't affected by him, Claire,'' retorted Leigh. "You're married, not dead. So what did he want, Michelle? Whatever it is, I volunteer."

"He's a lobbyist," said Michelle. "His name is Steve Saraceni and he represents Allied Medical Technologies. He wants to take the committee to lunch next week and talk about a hazardous waste incinerator."

Claire groaned. Leigh looked disappointed. "Hazardous waste? How gross! Still, he's so gorgeous he might even be able to make that sound romantic."

Leigh's rhapsodizing increased Michelle's sense of disconcertment. After all, her reaction to Steve Saraceni hadn't been much different. And now even Claire, a starry-eyed newlywed, was chiming in with appreciative remarks about Saraceni's incredible sex appeal. His effect on women was dynamite indeed, and Michelle knew he couldn't help but be aware of it. She shifted uncomfortably, longing for a change of subject.

Leigh wasn't. "He wasn't wearing a wedding ring," she noted. "If he were married, you can bet his wife would insist on one. That means he's single, he's available! And so am I!"

"So is Michelle," Claire added dampeningly. "And she's the one on the committee he's lobbying. She's the one going to lunch with him."

Michelle felt her cheeks turn pink. "Have you two ever heard the term 'conflict of interest'? We haven't really needed to worry about it because Ed is a junior senator and doesn't have enough influence or power for the lobbyists to come around much. But—"

"Conflict of interest," Claire interrupted, grinning. "It sounds exciting, forbidden, passionate. Go for it, Michelle."

Michelle smiled in spite of herself. In a moment, she was laughing along with the others. After all, Claire was deliberately being outrageous. Everyone in Senator Dineen's office knew how hardworking, loyal and dedicated Michelle was to her job. If there was a single staffer in Harrisburg who wouldn't ever need to worry about becoming embroiled in a conflict of interest, that person would be Michelle Carey.

Steve returned to his office to find his cousin Saran painting her nails while simultaneously talking on the telephone. She had the receiver tucked into the curve between her neck and shoulder and from her giggles, Steve was absolutely certain that the call had nothing at all to do with business.

He suppressed a groan. The family had foisted Saran upon him four months ago, after she'd completed a year of business school that had allegedly prepared her for office work. In what type of office, Steve had never been able to ascertain but he had dutifully created this job of receptionist for her, according to the family credo: Saraçenis stick together. Bonded like glue, Steve often added, not always facetiously.

He heaved a sigh. "Get off the phone, Saran."

Saran scowled, but quickly obeyed. "Heather and I were making plans to go see Boiled in Oil in Philly next weekend," she told him eagerly. "And you'll never guess what, Steve? Heather knows a girl who knows Boiled in Oil's drummer. She's going to get us introduced to the band!"

"Meeting *Boiled in Oil*. Now there's a dream come true," Steve said dryly.

"You're too old to appreciate them. You baby boomers are stuck way back in time with, like, the Rolling Stones."

"I wouldn't have appreciated a heavy metal punk catastrophe like *Boiled in Oil* at any age, Saran. I happen to have taste."

"Not in music—or in women," Saran shot back. "I've met some of the babes you go out with. They actually make *me* look smart! No wonder you don't want to get married. Those airheads you date are as far removed from wife material as—as—"

"—as Boiled in Oil's noise is from real music," Steve finished triumphantly. He headed toward his office.

"I told Heather that you're boring and old but she still thinks you're hot," Saran called after him. "She wants to go out with you really bad. Want to come to Confetti's with us tonight? That hot new team from WTXH radio are going to be the DJs."

Steve considered spending an evening with Saran and her friend Heather and decided that he would rather be—well, boiled in oil. "Thanks, but I'm busy tonight."

Sitting in his office, it struck him that for years he had been dating girls the age that Saran and Heather were now. In fact, Heather, with her blatantly sexy, flashy style, could even be categorized as just his type. For some inexplicable reason, the revelation horrified him. He was fourteen years older than Saran; he'd always thought of her as a little kid. So wouldn't that make girls her age just kids, too?

Like a man drowning, he saw his dating life flash before his eyes. Young women of twenty, twenty-one, twenty-two, used to be his peers. Now, suddenly, he was a man who dated little girls?

Inexplicably, he thought of Michelle Carey. She was no little girl, though she was young for the position she held. In fact, the entire Dineen staff were in their twenties and early thirties, a hardworking, ambitious and tight-knit group who were not yet well known among the state capital's political establishment.

Steve had done some research to learn more, but for some unfathomable and disconcerting reason, he'd found his interest focused more on Senator Dineen's aide, Michelle Carey, than the senator himself.

She was a serious career woman and she dressed to prove it. The two times he'd seen her, today and last week while on a prior reconnaissance mission, she had been wearing practical, businesslike dark suits that looked like they'd sprung from that decade-old office primer *Dress for Success*.

It was a look Steve detested. Women should dress like women in alluring fabrics, eye-pleasing colors, and figure-enhancing styles. He envisioned Michelle in a short, tight, red leather mini and a soft, clingy sweater. The swift, scorching heat of arousal stirred in his groin.

Which brought him to another thing he'd learned about Michelle. Regardless of the way she dressed, she was a knockout. She had thick blond hair he would love to loosen from the tight, practical styles she favored. He wanted to see those dark golden tresses falling sexily around her shoulders—or spread out on his pillow as he leaned over her in the quiet hush of his bedroom.

He pictured her beautiful china blue eyes blazing with passion for him. He wanted to taste her soft, tempting mouth, to feel her lips under his. Her luscious, curvaceous body tantalized his imagination. Her feminine appeal and shapeliness could not be disguised, not even by those prim and proper office uniforms of hers.

He was attracted to her. And for Steve Saraceni, a sexual attraction quickly blazed into a full-blown affair. There was every reason to suppose this one could, too. Michelle was attracted to him, too, he knew it. He had seen the look in her blue eyes and read it for what it was—awareness, attraction, desire. He was too experienced not to recognize the most subtle signs from the most reserved woman.

Normally he would act at once. A phone call. A strategically thoughtful little gift. An invitation to dinner. Candlelight, wine, candy and flowers—they might be cliché but they never failed. He was a virtuoso at cultivating the attraction, escalating the sexual tension. When he carefully

turned up the heat, they proceeded directly to the bedroom.

His campaign was so familiar to him, he could conduct it
by rote. Lately he had been.

But this was different; *she* was different. He had always
been careful not to become involved with any woman whose
path crossed his in the legislative/lobbyist world. There was
his business life and there was his social life, which he regarded as two very separate entities. Steve didn't believe in
mixing the two. He'd seen the result when others had.

A serious conflict of interest could arise and lead to mu-
tually damaged careers. But there was an even greater danger when a man and a woman with education, business and
other common interests came together in an affair. *Marriage!* Steve had seen it happen time and time again and
vowed it was not going to happen to him—at least not for a
long, long time. Marriage would interfere with his work, his
life, his golf game!

It hadn't been too hard to maintain his resolve. He admired his female colleagues in the political world; he respected them and enjoyed their company. But he wasn't
attracted to them. Michelle Carey made him rethink his
pledge of not mixing business with pleasure. Suddenly the
prospect seemed tempting, not foolish. Exciting, not unthinkable. Even the inherent danger of it appealed.

But he didn't reach for the phone to make the call that
would kick off his official courtship campaign. Steve Saraceni was cool and calculating, a man not driven by impulse
or passion. He would give himself time to see if his attraction to Michelle Carey was merely a passing trifle. He
wouldn't see her until the committee lunch and if he still
wanted her, then he would decide whether or not to pursue
her.

Smiling, feeling pleased with himself, he called a client
with an update on the House reaction to their most recent
proposal. Thoughts of Michelle, women and sex were

promptly evicted from his mind. Nothing distracted Steve
Saraceni from the business at hand.

The committee was unable to accept Steve's invitation to
lunch until the following week. He entertained them in style
at Rillo's, Harrisburg's top-ranked restaurant, located on
the west shore. Rillo's marvelous food, generous portions
and lively, bustling atmosphere made it a favorite among the
capital crowd. Even Governor George Lindow was often
spotted there.

Michelle ordered one of the house specialties, swordfish
steamed with vegetables, a lunch far removed from the
sandwich and piece of fruit she usually brown-bagged at her
desk. She wasn't near Steve at the table. He had seated
himself by the key committee members, those wielding the
most influence, which she definitely was not. But she found
herself watching and listening to him through most of the
meal. He fascinated her.

Steve was the perfect host, chatting with each of the
members about a wide variety of subjects. He was well
versed in everything. Books—he'd read all the bestsellers;
movies—he'd seen all the latest ones; and sports—he could
discuss any sport and any team and was a wealth of information about the upcoming Super Bowl. In fact, he had
tickets for the big game. He made a few dry remarks about
the drubbing he had taken during his blessedly short college football career.

"I did the team a favor by leaving," he said with a wry
grin. "My replacement turned out to have the most tal-
ented hands in college football and Penn State had their
choice of bowl bids that year. I still get thank-you notes
from Coach Paterno."

Michelle watched and listened as he deftly engaged the
committee leaders in a discussion of the bill. He had a
smooth, sure presentation. His arguments for choosing Allied Medical Technologies Incorporated seemed so logical,

so practical and advantageous for all involved that it seemed almost irrational not to give them what they wanted here and now.

But there were no promises or commitments made, and Steve didn't seem to expect any. He graciously picked up the substantial tab and anyone observing the warm and friendly goodbyes at the table would assume they were a group of old pals who'd gotten together for a lunchtime reunion.

He didn't single out Michelle in any way. His attention remained focused on the key members. She was rather relieved, remembering her embarrassingly girlish response to him in her office, but she also felt strangely disappointed.

What did you expect? she mocked herself. That a man like Steve Saraceni—cool, smooth, devastatingly handsome *and* good at his job—would jeopardize this opportunity, one he was paying for, to devote time to her, the one committee member who was merely a liaison, the one member with no vote, power or influence? Why would he? Why should he?

Why hadn't he?

She was still feeling a little flat when she returned to her desk. When her telephone rang, she picked it up. Accessibility was a point of pride with Senator Dineen. Everybody who worked in his office answered their own phones, with the exception of the senator himself, of course.

"Michelle, this is Steve Saraceni."

He didn't have to identify himself, she'd known his voice at once. Her breath caught. "Yes?"

"How do you think it went?" he asked exuberantly. He sounded so cheerful, so hopeful. His open candor struck her as charming. No subtly smooth ploys here, he went straight to the heart of the matter.

She smiled as she told him, "The general consensus is that you did an excellent job of explaining your client's proposal in laymen's terms. Everyone agreed that you were credible and didn't try to oversell."

Had she said too much? Michelle wondered at once. Was it proper to relay the committee's response? She'd responded as she would to a friend. But as an aide to a lobbyist... Michelle bit her lip. She was on uncharted waters here.

Credibility. It was the highest compliment a lobbyist could be paid. On the other end of the line, Steve was beaming.

"I'm glad. Thanks, Michelle." He paused. "Michelle, I'm sorry I didn't get to spend much time with you at lunch. In fact, I hardly had a chance to talk to you at all. I hope you understand. I had to give AMT, Inc., their money's worth."

"Of course." She sounded both excited and puzzled. Why had he called her?

Steve could read voice inflections as skillfully as he could interpret body language and word nuances. What he heard in hers pleased him.

"I've been looking forward to seeing you again," he continued. "As a matter of fact, I've had to talk myself out of calling you several times these past two weeks. I didn't want to place you in an uncomfortable position or have you think that I was trying to cultivate a personal relationship with you for my own professional gain."

Why, it was true, Steve realized, more than a little surprised. Until this moment, he thought he'd stayed away because he had put his attraction for her on hold, to be considered at his own convenience. Now it seemed that he'd actually had another, more altruistic motive, one considering *her*.

That was unlike him. Uneasily, he began to fiddle with the pens and pencils in the leather cylinder that held them.

Michelle's stomach dropped, as if she were on the double-loop roller coaster at a nearby amusement park. "I wouldn't think that, Steve," she said softly.

Steve cleared his throat. This was beginning to get sticky. Now was the time to lighten things up with a cleverly glib remark. His brain had stockpiled thousands to fit any situation.

Except this one, it seemed. "I'm glad," he heard himself say. Which hardly qualified for clever or glib. Help, he thought. He felt mired in mental quicksand.

Michelle came to his rescue. "I didn't know that you went to Penn State," she said, mercifully taking the conversation in a different direction. "I did, too."

"I know," said Steve. Relieved, he continued expansively, "I saw your diploma in your office. Did you happen to know my sister, Jamie Saraceni? She went to Penn State, too. She would've been a class or two ahead of you, I think. Majored in library science. She's married now. In fact, she just had a baby boy last month, two weeks before Christmas. His name is Matthew Albert Marshall."

Good Lord, he needed a clamp on his tongue! Steve grimaced. What was the matter with him? He wasn't normally given to long, free association monologues.

But Michelle didn't seem to mind. In fact, she gamely replied, "A new little nephew, how nice. No, I didn't know your sister, but of course, Penn State's main campus is an enormous place."

"Jammed to capacity with students," Steve agreed. "Remember those lines at the bookstore the beginning of each term?"

"I'll never forget them! How about the lines in the dining halls?"

Some things in State College remained the same, whatever the year and the class, and Michelle and Steve reminisced about their alma mater and the classes, professors, social life and sports. There had been some changes in their old college town, and they discussed those, too. The conversation was so enjoyable to them both that it continued for more than half an hour.

Then Michelle was interrupted by Claire. "I hate to bother you, Michelle, but you were going to read over this draft before we showed it to Ed, and he's due here in about fifteen minutes.''

And Steve was interrupted by Saran. ''Steve, there's this guy who's been waiting around to see you for the past twenty minutes and he's getting awfully hyper. Are you going to see him or should I tell him to get lost?''

''Oh my goodness, the draft!'' Michelle exclaimed. ''Claire, I'll get to it right away.''

''Good Lord! I forgot all about my appointment with the chief counsel to the party caucus!'' gasped Steve. ''Saran, do *not* tell him to get lost!''

''I guess we lost track of the time,'' Michelle said sheepishly over the phone to Steve.

''And I accused my cousin of conducting marathon telephone calls!'' Steve murmured, completely nonplussed. He had never, ever forgotten an appointment! Nothing distracted him from his work, particularly not a *woman*. He'd always consigned women to his leisure time when they would not interfere with anything important.

Yet, even now, both were oddly loath to hang up.

''Maybe we could—'' Michelle said at the same time that Steve was saying, ''Would you like to—''

They both paused and laughed awkwardly.

''You first,'' said Steve.

''No, really. You go ahead,'' insisted Michelle.

''I was going to ask if you'd like to continue this discussion over dinner sometime?''

''Yes,'' she replied quickly. Probably too quickly, but Michelle didn't care.

''I know this is short notice, but what about Friday night?'' He did some swift mental calculations. He had a date, of course; he always had a date on Friday nights. Saturdays, too. But he'd never had a problem with breaking dates if something else—some*one* else—came along.

''Friday night is fine,'' Michelle said breathlessly. A Friday night date, now that was a rarity for her. Usually she rented a video and watched it with her cat, both of them crashing on the sofa after her sixty-hour-plus work week. Her job consumed most of her energy and too many hours for her to pursue much of a social life.

"Would Alfred's Victorian be all right?" He named a popular restaurant in a restored Victorian mansion, which had carefully preserved the luxurious, old-fashioned ambience. He already had reservations there for Friday at eight.

"Oh, that would be very nice," Michelle exclaimed. She knew the place. Senator Dineen treated his staff to an annual Christmas party there. But the romantic atmosphere would be entirely different with Steve instead of the office gang. A tremor of anticipation shook her.

"Great. I'll pick you up around seven." That meant erasing the name already written in his pocket calendar, but that was okay. He always used pencil, never pen, for his social engagements. Pencil was freedom and subject to change; ink was permanence, commitment and obligation.

He wasn't aware that he'd reached for a pen to write in Michelle's name until he saw the ink on his pocket calendar's Friday square. He felt slightly spooked for a moment, but swiftly disregarded it. He'd never found any relevance or credence in so-called Freudian slips. As far as he was concerned, they were as hocus-pocus as Ouija boards, tea leaves and palm reading.

And *chain letters*. He grimaced as he crumpled up the one he'd just opened and tossed it into the trash just as a gum-chewing Saran led the irate chief counsel into his office.

Two

Steve timed his arrival at Michelle's apartment for a strategic 7:13 p.m., not too late to be insulting yet definitely, deliberately not on time. Arriving early, of course, was unthinkable. It could be disastrous if a woman got the idea that he was chomping at the bit to be with her!

Michelle was running late. The ramifications of a five o'clock phone call had kept her in the office till nearly 6:30. Traffic was unusually snarled and she burst into her apartment at two minutes past seven, grateful that Steve hadn't arrived yet.

She groaned when the doorbell rang at 7:13. If only he'd been a little later! As it was, she had just pulled on her dress, she was shoeless, and hadn't even started on her hair or makeup.

"Hi! I'm so sorry I'm not ready yet," Michelle greeted him distractedly at the door. "It was crazy at the office today and I had to stay late. And naturally, traffic was the worst because I was in a hurry."

She reminded herself to smile. This was a date. She was supposed to be anticipating a good time, not feeling harassed.

So much for his tactical arrival, Steve noted dryly. She hadn't even noticed the time, unless it was to hope he'd be later. He was slightly disconcerted. His dates were usually ready and waiting for him at the door when he made his shrewdly timed arrival.

"If you want to help yourself to something to drink, I'll hurry and finish getting dressed," Michelle said, already heading toward the bathroom.

Steve blinked. He'd hardly gotten a glimpse of her. She'd come and gone so quickly, she had been little more than a blur. He glanced around the small living room. It was neat but undistinguished, furnished with garage sale pieces mixed with the kind of new furniture sold in discount warehouses. His own place was similarly furnished. Who wanted to spend time and money on decorating? Leave that to the married couples who seemed to thrive on such projects.

He looked at the collection of picture frames grouped on an end table and wondered who all the smiling faces were. If Michelle was around, he could have asked her, but she had immediately made herself unavailable. Steve frowned. He wasn't accustomed to being left to his own devices in a woman's apartment. Usually, he was *smothered* with attention.

It occurred to him that, for the women he usually dated, his appearance was the highlight of their day. Maybe even their week. His dates were the living-for-the-weekend kind of girls who had little or no interest in their jobs, girls who just wanted to have fun. His arrival signaled the beginning of their real life.

But Michelle had a job that she took seriously, one that involved her and engaged her. She had a life that extended beyond the fun of the weekend. She hadn't taken the afternoon off to do her hair and her nails or to shop for a new outfit to wear for him. He knew from his own work experience that if she had stayed late at the office, her attention had been on the project at hand, not on him.

Such were the drawbacks of dating a career woman. No wonder he'd always avoided them. Feeling neglected, he walked into the small kitchen and opened the refrigerator. She'd offered him something to drink—which he had to fix himself!—and he had his choice of diet soda, fruit juice, or milk. There was no imported beer or ale. No wine, not even a wine cooler. What a way to kick off an evening! Sulking a little, he poured himself a glass of cranapple juice.

He reached into the pocket of his sport coat and pulled out a tiny stuffed toy lion wearing a blue and white shirt and cap with the letters PSU on the front. It was the Nittany Lion, Penn State's mascot. He'd purchased it as a memento of his and Michelle's first long talk on the phone. Steve set it on the kitchen counter to surprise her.

The surprise was on him when a dark, sleek Siamese cat appeared out of nowhere to leap on the counter and snatch the small toy in its mouth. "Hey!" Steve demanded in a whisper. "You can't have that!" He was careful not to raise his voice. It was most unbecoming to scold a date's pet.

But Burton the cat was undeterred. He ran under the living room sofa, carrying his prey. Once safely ensconced there, he began to meow pitifully. His routine, which included all of Michelle's attention when she returned from work plus tidbits from her dinner, had been disrupted by her late arrival and frantic preparations to dress. Worse, there was no dinner, only the dry cat food in his bowl.

Steve grimaced. He knew cats; there were eight of them living in the Saraceni home in New Jersey. They were masters at hiding and escape. He wouldn't get the stuffed animal back until the Siamese decided to relinquish it.

Burton continued to yowl and Michelle scurried out of the bathroom, still shoeless. Steve didn't kid himself. It was the cat, not him, who'd brought her running.

"Poor Burton, poor Burtie boy," she crooned. "What's the matter? Where are you?"

"He's under the sofa. He took one look at me and ran," Steve said wryly.

"Burton is shy around strangers," Michelle said apologetically. "He gets nervous, he's a little high strung."

"He's also a thief," Steve murmured, but Michelle didn't hear him. She was already on her hands and knees in front of the sofa, talking softly to the cat, trying to coax him out.

Steve glanced at her, swallowed, then steadfastly fixed his gaze on her. For the first time that evening he had a chance to see her, really see her, and he liked what he saw. She was wearing a short black stretch velvet dress, a pull-over sheath with long sleeves and a wide neckline. Cabochon-shaped faux stones in bright multicolored hues studded the material and glimmered in the lamplight.

The effect was dazzling but Steve was appreciating the sight of her long shapely legs encased in sheer dark hose and tucked under her even more. His eyes lingered on her derriere, rounded and pert and accentuated by both her position and the stretchy fabric of the dress. He found himself smiling.

Suddenly his unheralded arrival, the uninspiring drink and the cat's theft of his gift were only minor irritants, something to good-naturedly shrug off. The sight of Michelle in that dress was an auspicious sign of a very memorable night, he was certain of it.

"Come on out, Burton." Michelle continued to sweet talk the cat, to no avail. "He's got something under there and he's chewing on it."

"Burton's captured himself a Nittany Lion," Steve said dryly. "Is he a Pitt fan or what?"

Looking confused, Michelle stood up, smoothing her dress with her hands.

Steve was still smiling. She really was a knockout! Her figure, contained but not concealed beneath those tailored suits she favored in the office, more than fulfilled its promise in that short, sexy black dress. Her blond hair fell loose and lustrous to her shoulders.

"I brought you a little mascot but Burton saw it first and carried it to his lair," explained Steve. "I think he's dining on it now."

"Oh, dear!" Michelle looked distressed for a moment, then began to laugh.

Steve stared at her, transfixed. He'd never seen her laugh like that. The sound warmed him and her face, her eyes— she was beautiful! He couldn't tear his eyes away from her.

"Well, I thank you for the thought and Burton thanks you for the gift, I'm sure," Michelle said, starting out of the living room again. "I'll get my shoes and my purse and we can be on our way."

She returned moments later wearing black velvet evening pumps with high, narrow heels and carrying a short black cardigan-style coat. "It occurred to me that I haven't been a very good hostess. I'm sorry I've been rushing around so much since you've arrived."

Why, she'd paid more attention to the cat than to Steve, Michelle acknowledged ruefully. Her dating/entertaining skills were definitely rusty. And perhaps she shouldn't have laughed when the cat swiped his gift? She sought to make amends. "It was so thoughtful of you to bring—"

"—the cat a present?" Steve finished, his dark eyes twinkling. "Next time I'll bring you something. And there's no need to apologize," he added gallantly. "You're well worth the wait." He took her coat from her, to assist her into it. "You look beautiful tonight, Michelle."

Michelle flushed with pleasure. "Thank you." The warmth in his eyes as he looked at her, the admiration in his voice made her feel beautiful. She sent a mental thanks to her stepsister Ashlinn for insisting that she buy this dress when the two of them had been shopping together in New York City last fall.

She turned to slip into her coat, slightly tilting her head so her hair fell forward. Steve stared at the soft vulnerable skin of her nape as a jolt of sexual electricity streaked through him. Impulsively he put the coat aside and laid his hands on her shoulders, drawing her back to him. He inhaled the alluring scent of her perfume and his mind clouded. Unable to resist, he touched his mouth to her nape.

Michelle shivered. She wasn't accustomed to being caressed. Intellectually, she knew she was probably quite vulnerable to even the simplest touch, but emotionally, physically she savored the feel of his lips against her sensitive skin, the strength of his strong fingers kneading her shoulders. She couldn't remember the last time she'd felt so feminine, so desirable. Maybe never. But she could feel the heat and power of Steve's desire against her. He wanted her! And instead of feeling nervous, she was thrilled.

Whether she turned of her own accord or Steve turned her around himself, Michelle wasn't sure, but somehow she was facing him. She gazed up at him and her breath caught in her throat. His eyes were dark, fiery and intense. She felt his gaze slide over her, her mouth, her breasts, her legs, assessing and admiring.

His head lowered to hers and her lips tingled with anticipation. The way he was looking at her, the way he was handling her was wildly exciting. It was the way of an experienced, confident man, a man who understood how to please and satisfy a woman.

Maybe too experienced and probably too confident. The cold voice of reality broke the sensual spell enveloping Michelle. She had always had a practical, down-to-earth streak that kept her strong and steady. Just when her thoughts veered toward the likes of a confession-magazine narrative, that prosaic little voice in her head inevitably brought her up short.

Giving her head a small shake, she pulled out of his embrace. "I don't think we—" she began.

"Of course. I understand," Steve said quickly. He frowned, confused. He'd touched her and come close to losing his head. An unsettling development. He liked being in control, he insisted on it. *You're no grabby adolescent,* he admonished himself. *Get a grip!*

"I know how much women hate having their makeup smeared at the beginning of the evening. I hope you'll accept my apology."

"Smeared makeup?" Michelle echoed, staring at him. Furthermore, he hadn't made an apology to accept. "You think that's why I—" She decided that she was offended. "My makeup had nothing to do with it. Even if I hadn't been wearing any, I would've called a halt because—I hardly know you and I don't make a practice of ... of kissing men I don't know."

"What about the men you do?"

"What?"

"Just a little joke," he said hastily. "Anyway, we weren't kissing."

Michelle blushed. "But we would have been if I hadn't—"

"Maybe. Maybe not," he interrupted, shrugging. "I might've called a halt to things, too, you know."

"Oh, of course. Out of concern for the state of my makeup," she drawled caustically.

Steve heaved a sigh. "Look, I know bickering is an effective way to diffuse sexual tension, but to be honest with you, I've never cared for it. I'm not the confrontational type."

"I'm not, either." Michelle stared at him, nonplussed. "Is—Is that what we were doing?"

"Afraid so. And I'm sorry about that women-and-their-makeup crack, too. It was insulting."

"As you intended," she said slowly. "My, you're good. You said it so ingenuously I thought you weren't aware of how insulting you were being."

"It's a talent of mine. Sort of goes with the territory."

"Disguising carefully aimed barbs as artless blurts of spontaneity." She looked dismayed. "In politics, I've learned to read between the lines but dealing with you seems to require reading between the words."

"And you're questioning whether or not I'm worth the time and the trouble," surmised Steve. "I know the feeling. I wondered the same thing about you when I first arrived and you weren't crawling all over me, panting with delight."

Her jaw dropped. "Is that the way your dates normally greet you?"

"Let's just say...yes."

"Oh." His honesty disarmed her. She remembered her hurried, distracted greeting to him. And then she'd left him alone with the irascible Burton! What could she say? She wasn't about to apologize for not jumping him at the door. For not panting with delight at the sight of him!

She cleared her throat. "Maybe this wasn't such a good idea. We, uh, obviously had different ideas about what kind of an evening this was going to be and—"

"Michelle, I decided that you definitely were worth the time and trouble," he cut in, his dark eyes blazing.

"Despite a lamentable lack of crawling and panting?" Her lips twitched.

Steve laughed. "Maybe it's time for a change."

It was also time to learn why he was captivated by that cautious half smile she was giving him, why he was intrigued by her reluctance to accede to his charm. He wasn't the sort of guy who thrived on the challenge and conquer of women who played hard to get. He went for the sure thing every time, as his disapproving sister Jamie continually pointed out to him. And what was so wrong with that? he'd often wondered. After all, he worked hard at his job. He certainly didn't want to expend any extra efforts on dating!

"Shall we proceed as planned?" he suggested. He reached out to smooth his hand along her arm, cupping her elbow in his palm.

Michelle's heart seemed to jump into her mouth, which had suddenly gone dry. His slightest touch seared her with a seductive heat that made her ache. She was going to have to be very careful around this man, this too handsome man who had been badly spoiled by all those nitwits who crawled all over him and panted with delight merely because he'd shown up.

But she nodded her acquiescence and allowed him to help her into her coat. Her decision had been made. She had always wondered if she would ever meet a man who interested and excited her as much as her job. Steve Saraceni did. He was worth her time and trouble.

The maitre d' at the restaurant knew Steve and deferentially escorted the couple to the second floor where cushioned banquettes were built into a turret. Lacy curtains ensured the diners' privacy. Candles flickered on the table and a haunting romantic ballad played softly in the background. It was the perfect setting for romance.

Maybe too perfect. When Steve reached over and covered her hand with his, Michelle quietly but carefully removed hers, using the pretext of arranging her napkin on her lap. It would be so easy to lose herself in the romantic atmosphere, to let Steve hold her hand and ply her with the excellent wine he'd ordered. But Michelle had never been one to take the easy way. She made a vow to keep her head.

But that didn't mean she couldn't enjoy the superb food and Steve's company. She was, very much. "I love their seafood bisque," Michelle said, sighing appreciatively as she inhaled its tantalizing aroma.

"Mmm, me, too," Steve agreed. "And my grandmother has given Alfred's northern Italian dishes her stamp of approval, although she remains firmly convinced that southern Italy is the gastronomical center of the world. I brought her here for dinner when she came to visit me and my cousin Saran.''

Michelle liked the way he smiled as he talked about his grandmother, his eyes warm with humor and affection. ''Was she born in Italy?''

Steve nodded. ''In San Vito on the Adriatic. Her family immigrated to the United States when she was two. They passed through Ellis Island. We took Grandma there after it reopened as a museum, and she swore she could remember her family's arrival there.''

''Maybe she could. I have some memories of being two. They're vague and sketchy but real.'' Michelle twisted her napkin in her lap. ''That was the year my parents were divorced. I remember sitting at the top of the stairs with my older sister and brothers, watching our father leave, carrying his suitcase. My sister picked me up and carried me into her bed. She was crying, but I wasn't. I guess I really didn't understand what was going on.''

Steve frowned. ''Divorce is hell on kids. My two nephews took it hard when their mother—that's my sister Cassie—split with their dad. It wasn't Cassie's fault,'' he added swiftly, loyally. ''Her husband got sick of being married and wanted out. Cassie and the kids moved in with our folks and Grandma.'' His frown deepened. ''The whole family thinks her ex, Wayne Blair, is something akin to the antichrist, but—'' he paused ''—the guy isn't evil, he just wasn't cut out for marriage. Wayne was a lousy husband and an indifferent father. He felt trapped, they didn't understand, everybody was miserable. He actually did Cassie and the kids a favor by leaving. They're happier and better off without him around.''

''That's his rationalization, I'm sure,'' murmured Michelle. ''Quite convenient and self-serving. And a whole lot easier than having to stick around, to grow up and make things work.''

Her remark rankled him. Though he disliked his former brother-in-law for hurting his sister, Steve had an uneasy feeling that he himself wouldn't fare much better in the husband-and-father role. He considered himself a born-free type with a congenital need for independence. Not a self-serving, rationalizing, immature type.

"Uh-oh. I just remembered why I never discuss serious topics, like divorce, on dates. Too emotional and controversial."

"Which would certainly put a damper on all that crawling and drooling you expect from your dates," Michelle said drolly.

Steve was startled. He wasn't used to being needled by his dates. Of course, he rarely—never?—dated anyone as intelligent as Michelle. "Panting," he corrected, grinning in spite of himself. Actually, he rather enjoyed her needling. "My dates crawl and pant. I draw the line at drooling."

She rolled her eyes. "Whatever. Anyway, you're right, there are some subjects that ought to be avoided during dinner. Traumatic childhood memories, for one." Her tone was light, but she shifted uneasily. "I don't know what possessed me to inflict mine on you." An embarrassing lapse, another sign of her moldering social skills, no doubt.

She quickly sought to make amends. "Look, it's starting to snow," she exclaimed, glancing out the window. Her smile and her voice were very bright. "I don't remember any of our esteemed area meteorologists predicting that. Don't tell me they're wrong again! Remember last year when they predicted a blizzard with at least ten inches accumulation and instead the day turned out to be fifty degrees and sunny?"

Steve knew it was his turn to chime in with an amusing anecdote about weather and the hapless foibles of those predicting it. Michelle was behaving exactly as he had directed, smiling brightly and chattering about bland generalities, keeping it light and impersonal. Why on earth did he have the perverse wish to revert to their earlier conversation, which had been emotional and revealing and entirely too personal? There was no need for him to know—no reason for him to wonder—

"What happened after your dad left?" he asked suddenly.

Michelle looked at him as if he'd grown another head. "I thought we agreed to talk about something else."

"Well, I—"

"There's no reason for you to politely pretend an interest in my distant past," she said dryly. "I don't even find it very interesting."

"I'm not politely pretending interest. I am interested. Why did your folks split up? Did your father decide he wasn't into marriage and kids, like Cassie's ex?"

"Oh, it wasn't that," she said quickly. "In fact, two years after the divorce, Daddy married a widow with three children. They adored him and he was devoted to them, too. My father is very much a family man. It was his career that broke up my parents' marriage. Dad was a career Army officer and Mom hated moving from post to post. She demanded that he give it up and he wouldn't. He couldn't. He'd been an Army brat himself and he loved the service."

"Mmm, that is a tough one. I can't see giving up my work for anyone or anything."

"Me, either. I never blamed my father for choosing the Army, but my mother never forgave him. She's still angry with him, even though she's been remarried to a perfectly nice man for the past twenty years."

"Whew! Talk about holding a grudge!"

"My sentiments exactly." Michelle shrugged. "Enough Carey family history. If we're swapping life stories, it's your turn to tell me more about the Saracenis."

"There's not much to tell. My parents were high school sweethearts who were born and raised in Merlton and are still living there. Grandma lives with them and so do Cassie and her two kids. My sister Jamie lives less than twenty minutes away with her husband and new baby." He shrugged. "It works for them, they're happy. But all that togetherness makes me claustrophobic. From the time I was in elementary school I wanted to get out, to have more, to do more, you know?"

"No." Michelle shook her head. "That's my dream life—an intact family in the same place, always there for you. My family is scattered all over the country and always has been."

So, she was looking to recreate what she'd lost so long ago? Steve gulped. Maybe he should've come up with a weather joke, after all. Instead he told another kind of joke, one currently making the rounds at the Capitol. If she'd heard it, she didn't let on and laughed appreciatively at the punch line.

The conversation seemed to naturally drift to less personal topics, most of it centering on the latest news and gossip circulating the state political scene. They found they had a number of acquaintances in common.

"I'm surprised we never met before this," Steve remarked after the waiter removed their salad plates.

"I don't do much socializing," Michelle confessed. "My work takes up so much of my time and energy, I don't have much left over for anything else." Which wasn't entirely true, she knew, but it was an acceptable excuse, one she used so often she was almost beginning to believe it herself.

"A good deal of my work is socializing," said Steve. He launched into his familiar spiel, the one he'd crafted for the frequent question, What exactly do lobbyists do?—even though Michelle hadn't asked it.

"Lobbyists go to fund-raisers, parties, luncheons, and dinners on behalf of charities, cultural groups, political action committees and campaigns. You name it and we're there, wherever the state legislators are. The name of the game is access. Even the appearance of access is a large part of the exercise.''

It sounded like a hellish existence to Michelle. ''Don't you ever get tired of it?''

''Tired of going out?'' Steve was flabbergasted by such a radical notion. ''Never! I can't think of the last time I spent an evening alone, sitting around my apartment. Hmm, maybe when I had the flu five years ago. I had to vegetate in front of the tube for three nights and I thought I'd go nuts. No, I love the night life. There isn't enough of it for me in Harrisburg so I drive into Philadelphia or Washington or New York City for ball games or parties or shows. I have friends there and—''

''Your social life spans four cities?'' Michelle interrupted, awed. ''And you have women that you date in each city?'' Did they greet him by crawling all over him and panting with delight. *In four different cities?*

A four-city social world. She could hardly take it in. Pride kept her from admitting to him that the span of her social life barely included the city limits of Harrisburg. But she had no trouble admitting to herself that this was her first and last date with Steve Saraceni. Even if he did manage to find time to sandwich her in between everybody else, everywhere else, what was the point? In the annals of dating, he'd achieved world-class status while she—didn't even qualify as a footnote!

There were too mismatched, too far apart, and not only geographically.

''I have *friends* in those particular cities,'' Steve reiterated. Looking across the table at Michelle, he could almost feel her withdrawal. ''That doesn't necessarily mean, uh, women I date,'' he added expediently.

But of course, it did, and they both knew it. He'd made a serious miscalculation in revealing the extent of his peripatetic social life, Steve realized ruefully. Michelle hadn't been impressed as his dates usually were. She was appalled!

Her expression, her tone of voice, her entire response reminded him of his sister Jamie's reaction to his rollicking tales of adventure. Terrific, he thought grimly. Until he'd met Michelle, his intransigent little sister had been the one person in the world he couldn't charm, the one person in the universe who didn't look upon him with favor and indulgence. Now, it seemed, there were two of them—Jamie *and* Michelle.

Weirdly enough, he'd always secretly wanted Jamie's approval. Even more unfathomable, he realized that he also wanted Michelle's. He wanted her to gaze at him the way she'd done earlier. He remembered the warmth in her smile when they'd talked about his grandmother and wanted to see it again.

He tried, he really tried. Since Michelle had reacted favorably to his grandmother, he reintroduced her as a topic, shamelessly recounting a plethora of Grandma-and-Steve stories.

Michelle listened politely, but remained aloof, untouched and uninvolved. And stayed that way for the rest of the meal. And though Steve was at his amusing, charming best, though he radiated what had heretofore been fail-safe appeal, she remained impervious to it, to him.

It wasn't easy for her. Only a stone could stay unmelted by those warm dark eyes of his, Michelle mused grimly, and so she concentrated on being one. She had to work hard at maintaining a cool smile when she wanted to laugh out loud at his often hilarious stories. She had to stay constantly on guard to keep from falling under the potent spell of his charm. He was so attentive, so eager to please her. Michelle was exhausted as they rose to leave. Remaining impassive to his winning ways had required extraordinary effort.

It was only the knowledge that countless women in four cities undoubtedly did *not* remain impassive or on guard, and succumbed regularly to those well-practiced winning ways of his, that strengthened her resolve.

The snow was falling, fast and thick, as they left the restaurant. A surprising amount had accumulated during the two-and-a-half hours they'd been inside. They watched a car skid on the snow-covered street while another spun its wheels futilely, trapped on an icy patch.

"This storm came up so fast, I guess it caught the road crews by surprise," observed Steve. "There's been no snow removal at all from what I can see."

Michelle glanced nervously at a car fishtailing around the corner. "Do you have snow tires or chains?"

"On my car?" He was aghast. "Not on a bet."

She gazed up and down the street at the cars slipping, sliding and stuck in the snow. And Mr. Macho scorned snow tires and chains. "Driving is going to be murder. We'll be lucky to get off this street."

"My car drives like a dogsled in snow," retorted Steve. He started down the front walk that the restaurant personnel had cleared with calcium chloride crystals.

Michelle followed, pulling the belt of her coat tighter. It wasn't a very warm coat, designed more for style than cold temperatures. As an icy blast of wind swirled snow around her, she thought longingly of her boxy blue and gray goose-down parka hanging in her closet. It even had a hood! If she were wearing it now, her hair wouldn't be whipping around her head, and her neck and earlobes would not be flash-frozen. But she had opted for this coat, to be attractive for Steve. On their first and last date. Michelle sighed gloomily.

Unlike the private walk, the sidewalks hadn't been cleared, and Michelle watched Steve tramp through the snow ahead of her. She glanced regretfully at her velvet shoes. They would never be the same after the block-long trek through the snow. Shivering, she prepared to step into one of Steve's footsteps to follow the trail he was blazing.

And then, suddenly, he was back at her side. Michelle, who'd ducked her head low against the howling wind, jerked it up in surprise. And then gasped as she felt herself being lifted off her feet. "Wha—what are you doing?"

"What's it look like?" growled Steve. "I'm carrying you to the car."

He skidded, but managed to regain his footing almost immediately. Unnerved, Michelle clutched him around the neck. "We're going to fall! Please, put me down!"

"We're not going to fall and I'm not putting you down. I'm going to carry you so you can't blame me for ruining your shoes like I ruined your evening."

"I'm not sure I understand," Michelle said stiffly. The wind sent a blast of snow in her face, cooling her flushed cheeks.

Steve trudged through the blizzard, carrying her, his breathing growing more labored but his jaw stubbornly set.

"I know you had a lousy time tonight, Michelle. You were simply going through the motions, putting in time and waiting for the evening to be over." It was a strong speech for a perennially cool, uninvolved, nonconfrontational kind of guy, but Steve was glad he'd said it. "Don't bother to deny it," he added.

"All right, I won't," Michelle said quietly.

They reached his car. Steve held her as he opened the door and deposited her inside, her shoes and feet dry and snow-free. His were soaked and cold. A less chivalrous soul might've dumped her in the snow—and with just cause. He brushed off the snow from the car before he stomped around to his side to get in, commending himself on his gallantry.

She hadn't denied that she was glad the evening was over, that she hadn't had a good time! He'd been half expecting her to tell him that he had been reading her all wrong and he was prepared to believe it. Unfortunately he had been right on target.

Neither said anything as the car's engine roared to life. Steve easily steered the car out of the parking space and into the street. The windshield wipers worked diligently to keep the glass free of snow, but the flakes were falling so thick and so fast that it was a losing battle.

"The visibility is horrible," Michelle said anxiously. "Do you think you should pull over and—"

"Do what? Sit in the car and freeze until it stops snowing? No thanks. I've never had any trouble driving in the snow. I don't anticipate any now."

He'd no sooner uttered the words when the car began to fishtail. "We're at that bad corner." Michelle gulped. "The one none of the other cars—" Her voice rose into a terrified squeak as the car shot across the road. A telephone pole was looming.

Three

Michelle glanced at Steve manipulating the steering wheel with both hands and pumping the brake with his foot before she covered her eyes and braced herself for the collision...which didn't occur.

"You can open your eyes now," Steve said tersely. "We're still on the road."

Michelle snapped her eyes open and she gazed around her. The pole was behind them and the car was hugging the curb, inching along as the snow continued to fall with blinding fury.

"You did it," she breathed. A powerful surge of relief made her feel giddy.

"Of course. Didn't I tell you this car drives like a dog-sled?" He didn't feel as calm and cool as he sounded. They'd missed that pole by mere inches. The adrenaline that had suffused his system, sharpening his reflexes and his dexterity in the emergency, began to slowly abate. He took a few deep breaths and tried to ignore the wild thundering of his heart.

"So that was 'mush' I heard you muttering under your breath?" Michelle teased. "That's odd, it sounded remarkably similar to a certain swear word." She was lightheaded from the near miss, she felt like giggling and weeping at the same time. Careening toward the inexorable wooden strength of a telephone pole could do that to a person.

Steve braked to a stop at a traffic light—or tried to. The car slid through the intersection, fishtailing crazily. Fortunately there were no other cars on the road, so it didn't matter that they spun around in a complete circle.

Michelle gasped. Steve muttered a few more words, which sounded nothing like the "mush" a sledmaster called to his dog team.

"Your place is closer, mine is across town," he gritted as he slowly, carefully pulled the car onto a highway whose lanes were obliterated by the snow. It looked like a vast arctic tundra rather than a four-lane road.

Michelle nodded, picturing her apartment, warm, safe—and stationary. "I wish we could teleport ourselves there," she said softly.

"Scared?"

"Completely rattled," she admitted.

"We'll make it." He reached over and patted her hand for a second before resuming his grip on the wheel.

The rest of the drive, which normally took twenty minutes, was filled with two hours of close calls and near misses. They watched a succession of hapless motorists spin, skid, and slide off the road as they proceeded at a snail's pace—and sometimes even slower. As the storm worsened, the number of abandoned cars alongside the road—and in one case, in the middle of it—increased, creating additional obstacles to be avoided.

They played the radio for a while, but the incessant weather bulletins, proclaiming the impassability of the roads and the admonitions to stay off them, irritated Steve and unnerved Michelle.

"Staying inside isn't an option," Steve finally snapped back at the hypermanic voice of the radio announcer who had once again cautioned motorists not to drive in the blizzard. "We're already out on the roads." He switched off the radio. "What's the point in listening to secondhand reports of how treacherous the roads are? We're experiencing them firsthand."

They rode in tense silence then, Steve concentrating his attention on keeping the car on the road, Michelle mentally willing him success in doing so. By the time he pulled the car into the snow-filled parking lot adjacent to her apartment building, both were exhausted from the dual strains of anxiety and tension.

Steve shifted gears in an attempt to pull the car closer to the building. The tires went around and around, but the Jag didn't move. He tried again, pressing the gas pedal harder. Again, nothing. The odor of friction-burning rubber assailed their nostrils as the wheels kept spinning. They were stuck on the ice, blocked in by the snow.

Steve cut the engine and leaned against the steering wheel. "Looks like our luck's run out," he said glumly.

"It doesn't matter, we made it!" Michelle exclaimed. "We're home!" A smile lit her face. "I don't mind admitting it now, but there were times, a lot of them in fact, when I didn't think we would ever get here. I thought we'd end up spending the night trapped in a ditch or wrapped around a pole. You drove—" she paused, searching for a superlative "—brilliantly," she finished exuberantly.

"So how do you feel about having this brilliant driver spend the night in your apartment?"

Michelle gaped at him, shocked.

Steve laughed slightly. "*You're* home, honey, not me. I've managed to get stuck in this stupid lot and it looks like I won't be going anywhere else tonight."

Michelle swallowed and said nothing. *He was going to have to spend the night in her apartment?* She'd been so profoundly relieved to be safely home, she hadn't had time to consider Steve's predicament. And her own!

"Guess I'm not so brilliant, after all, huh? Although there are those who might argue that getting myself marooned so I have to sleep over at your place is a brilliant strategy."

His attempted joke fell flat. Michelle glanced at him. He looked so tired, as drained as she felt. And no wonder—he'd just put in two hours of perilous driving.

"I know you didn't do it deliberately," Michelle said quietly, staring sightlessly at the snow whipping around the car. The heat inside was rapidly dissipating since he'd turned off the engine. She shivered.

"I certainly didn't. I'm not the kind of guy who hangs around where I'm not wanted. And you made it clear tonight that you don't want to be around me."

Maybe it was the flatness in his voice or the absence of expression in his usually expressive face. Or perhaps it was the bond that forms between those who have faced an exhausting, difficult trial together. Whatever it was, Michelle felt guilt streak through her. "I didn't mean to give you that impression," she said softly. "I'm sorry if I was rude. I was trying to be polite this evening. I thought I'd succeeded."

"Oh, you were polite, all right. You smiled at all the right times, you nodded and came up with correct responses the conversation required. Except that you were on automatic pilot while you were doing it." Steve frowned. "I can tell the difference between what's real and what's faked, Michelle. Both in and out of bed."

"How can you tell if a woman is faking in bed?" Michelle blurted out, completely bewildered by his unexpected candor. "Every magazine article I've ever read on the subject says a man can never tell." She wanted to recall the words the moment she said them. Blushing, she felt hot all over, despite the windchill factor.

He arched his dark brows. "Do you believe everything you read, Michelle? If you do, then you believe that Elvis is still alive, that Hitler was really a woman—"

"What?"

"According to a tabloid headline I read in a supermarket line, Hitler was really a woman. It's World War II's best-kept secret."

Michelle couldn't help but laugh at that outlandish tale.

"The lesson here is don't believe everything you read," Steve said silkily. "And I can always tell when a woman is faking in bed, no matter what the magazines say."

Her smile abruptly vanished. Any prior sympathy she'd had for him dissolved just as rapidly. "Well, if any man can, I'm sure you're the one. You've certainly had enough experience, haven't you? All those women, in all those cities?"

"Not that again!" Steve groaned. "That's when our evening started going off the track, isn't it? When I mentioned that I had a life outside Harrisburg?"

"A life outside Harrisburg? That's a shamefully bland understatement! But you're very good at shading the truth—or sidestepping it altogether. *Putting a new slant on it* is the lobbyist term for that particular talent, I believe."

Steve heaved an exasperated sigh. "Michelle, I—"

"But I have a bit of advice for you that you might want to keep in mind," Michelle cut in. She wasn't going to stop now, she was on a roll. "It could prove useful for all those future dates of yours."

Steve was well aware that advice was inevitably scathing criticism when it came from a disapproving woman. He braced himself for it.

Michelle did not disappoint him. "These days, boasting about an active, non-monogamous *social* life is analogous to walking around with a sign saying Warning—Research

Lab Volunteer for the Communicable Disease Center. Thinking, discerning women will *not* be enchanted.''

"I've always been careful!" Steve protested. "Before safe sex became a catchword, I practiced it. From the time I was in high school, my idea of hell was a knocked-up girl at my door telling me that I was officially eligible for a card and a pair of socks on Father's Day. Bam—end freedom, begin family life. I've always taken care to make sure that doesn't happen."

"I commend you on your self-protective efforts," Michelle inserted with a saccharine smile. "But—"

"But you have more *advice?*" Steve interrupted, sounding aggrieved. "Why do women always feel free to take potshots at single men? It's perennially open season on us."

"Maybe it's because women don't like to feel that we're merely one among many. Fungible. As interchangeable as pennies in a jar. And men like you make us feel that way. Not unique, not special. Just a body and from your point of view, preferably an accommodating one."

"I guess it would be in poor taste to tell you that your body is definitely special? That I could make you feel things you've never felt before—unique could apply—if you'd care to be, uh, accommodating?"

He flashed a charming, coaxing smile. Michelle was neither charmed nor coaxed out of her increasing irritation. It didn't help that she knew he was teasing. For some inexplicable reason his refusal to take her seriously angered her. Far more than it should.

She knew that, too, and it made her even angrier. "I can see we've used up the sixty seconds you allot for any kind of serious conversation. Now it's back to the innuendoes and the flirting and the smooth little jokes. If you don't mind— and even if you do—I'm opting out of this round."

She flung open the car door. A strong gust of wind blew an icy blast of snow into the car, half blinding her. Michelle pushed herself out of the car, gasping as her feet plunged into several inches of cold, wet snow. A moment later, Steve was beside her.

He hooked one arm around her waist and together the two of them trudged toward the building. It was too cold and too windy to try to talk. All their energy was directed to battling the ferocious wind. By the time Steve pulled open the thick glass door and they entered the vestibule of the building, Michelle was gasping for breath. She'd been leaning on Steve to keep her balance along the icy walk. His strength had kept her upright and afoot during the hazardous trek.

"So much for your shoes," Steve said, staring at her soaked velvet pumps. Not that he could've carried her from the car; the force of the wind and depth of the snow would have prevented him from repeating his earlier chivalrous deed. And in the mood Michelle was in, she might've slugged him if he'd tried.

Michelle stamped her feet to shake the excess snow from them and Steve stared, riveted by the long, sleek length of her legs, so shapely and seductive in the sheer, smoky hose. He had to forcibly drag his gaze away.

"It's so much worse since we left the restaurant," Michelle murmured as she looked out the glass door at the awesome fury of the blizzard.

Steve followed her gaze. The storm showed no signs of abating. The winds were increasing to gale force and the snowfall was thicker and heavier than any he'd ever seen. "Damn, I really am stuck here for the night." It would be a first for him—spending the night with a sexy, desirable woman who found him as appealing as infectious waste. He stifled a groan.

"Did you think you'd be able to charm Mother Nature into winding down the storm for you?" It was supposed to be a joke, but Michelle's tone was more acerbic than she'd intended. The reality of the situation had just fully impacted on her. *Steve Saraceni was going to spend the night in her apartment.*

Steve frowned. "Can we call a truce in the hostilities?" He watched Michelle brush the snow from her coat. Her cheeks were cherry red, which had the effect of making her eyes an even deeper, brighter blue. Snowflakes glistened on her silky thick blond tresses. She was lovely, so fresh and classy. So elegantly sexy. Desire pierced him, and his body tightened. Impulsively he reached out and caught one golden lock between his fingers.

Michelle shot him a look and quickly moved away, out of his reach.

"There's snow in your hair," he said lamely. "I was only trying to brush it off."

"It will melt, thank you," Michelle said coolly. She started up the stairs.

Steve followed her. Why did she have to be so attractive? he silently lamented. Worse, why did he have to be so attracted to her? Her personality was certainly off-putting enough. She was prickly, cool, guarded and disapproving. Certainly nothing like the bouncy, cheerful, giggling girls he normally enjoyed in his leisure hours. *They* wouldn't even know what the Communicable Disease Center was!

Michelle and Steve climbed to the second floor and walked past an elevator on the way to her door. "You prefer cold, drafty stairwells with steep steps to the convenience of an elevator?" he asked. "It figures!"

"That elevator is notoriously slow and it's unreliable, too," Michelle explained crisply. "Everybody who lives in the building avoids it whenever possible."

She removed her key from her small purse.

"May I?" Steve asked smoothly, reaching for the key. He had long ago choreographed a sexy routine of unlocking the door with one hand while caressing his date with the other. The symbolism of the act heightened the anticipation and...

"I can do it," Michelle said dampeningly. She opened the door, no assistance required.

The apartment was dark and chilly, and Michelle scurried about the living room, turning up the heat and switching on every lamp. "You can sleep on the sofa," she told him, indicating the well-worn, rust-colored, U-shaped sofa. The cat was sprawled full-length in the middle of it.

"Terrific. A sectional sofa. Should be comfortable, particularly when the sections slide apart—which they invariably do when anyone lies down on them. But, hey, I'm not complaining. I'll have the cat to keep me warm."

Michelle fought to suppress a grin. Instinct warned her that laughing with him could be dangerous. Laughter dissolved barriers. It was far safer for her defenses to remain intact around him. "As you can see, I'm not really set up for overnight guests." Her voice was as rigid as her stance.

"Well, believe me, honey, I never intended on being one."

"Should I be insulted or flattered by that radical departure from your usual *modus operandi?*"

"Neither. I was, uh, shading the truth a bit." Smiling, Steve caught both her hands in his. "In all honesty, my *modus operandi* was right on track. From the moment I saw you in that dress, I had high hopes of being invited to stay over—but not on the sofa. In your bedroom." He lifted her palm to his mouth and pressed his lips against the warm center. "Care to rethink the sleeping arrangements, sweetie?"

Sweetie! Grimacing, Michelle pulled her hand away. "No."

Steve shrugged and flopped down next to the cat. "Oh well, it was worth a try. And admit it, you really would've been insulted if I'd hadn't made a single play for you."

Michelle stared at him, off balance once more. "That's all? You're giving up?" Could it possibly be this easy? She'd been feeling increasingly anxious and vulnerable since they'd entered the apartment . . . and rightfully so. A woman alone in her apartment with a man she really didn't know at all that well, and with date rape on the rise . . .

She eyed him warily. "You aren't going to . . . to make a serious pass at me?"

"I'll be glad to, if you give me the signal. Otherwise, consider my token attempt the pass of the night. I don't believe in forcing myself on a woman, Michelle. If she says no, I respect that."

Inordinately relieved, Michelle sank down onto the sofa beside him. "I'm glad to hear that. I wasn't looking forward to having to fight you off tonight."

"That would be a first for me," Steve said dryly. "I've never experienced having a woman fight me off."

Michelle gazed at him, unable to tear her eyes away. He really was a marvelous-looking man with those dark good looks and solidly masculine build. Her pulses fluttered oddly. "I suppose for you, the reverse applies," she said thoughtfully. "All those panting, eager dates of yours—*you* probably have to fight *them* off."

"To keep them from having their wicked way with me?" Steve laughed. "Let's not go into that. Suffice to say, that I understand no means no. And on the brighter side—yes means yes."

"So if a woman says yes, you'll take her to bed, but it doesn't really matter either way to you, does it?" Michelle frowned quizzically. "You're awfully nonchalant about all of this. I thought making conquests was serious business to men like you."

Steve leaned back against the sofa cushions and stretched his legs, resting his feet on the low, wide coffee table. "You're thinking of those neurotic types whose self-worth depends on whether or not they can lure women into bed with them. They usually do everything in their power to make the women fall in love with them, too—it's all part of their sick little ego-boosting game. Women make a big mistake by lumping all single men into the same category. There are major differences between those needy, insecure jerks and us confident, happy, independent guys. Those creeps give the rest of us a bad name."

He leaned toward her, his dark eyes intense. "I don't need a woman's capitulation to affirm my masculinity or to build my self-esteem. I'm very satisfied with myself and my life. I have my work and lots of interests, I have friends and family and I relish my freedom. I'm not looking for love and I've never pretended otherwise. I like women, I enjoy being with them, and I just want to have a good time."

Michelle regarded him archly. "Are you always this honest with the women you, uh, *date?* Are you always so upfront about your intentions—or the lack of them?"

Steve shrugged, grinning. "I don't usually talk this much with the women I, uh, *date.*" He mimicked her inflection perfectly. "We're usually doing something, like dancing or watching a movie or a ball game." He paused. "Or other things."

Other things. One could only imagine what that might include. Michelle tried to will away the flush of color that stained her cheeks. Unsuccessfully. "You don't have to elaborate," she said sternly.

"Before you condemn me out of hand, try to understand. I talk all day, all week long, remember? All lobbyists do is talk; it's the chief tool of the trade. I get so sick of talking. The last thing I want is to have to *talk* to my dates. In my spare time, I need a break from talking."

"So you date idiots whose conversation is limited to exclamations like 'oh, wow' and 'cool'?" guessed Michelle.

"Well, idiots is a bit harsh, but essentially, you've got the picture."

"I suppose it's never crossed your mind that there's a difference between lobbying and meaningful conversation. Or that you might actually enjoy talking with your dates if you chose women capable of intelligent conversation?"

His dark eyes gleamed. "Mmm, now there's a radical notion."

"Wait a minute, it just occurred to me. When you asked me out, did you assume that *I* was a bubblebrain who wouldn't mentally tax you?" Michelle was indignant. "You did, didn't you?"

"No, no! I knew you were different!"

"You're right on cue with that self-serving line." She gave him a speaking glance. "I hope you don't think I'm stupid enough to believe you."

"But it's true, Michelle. I really did enjoy talking to you on the phone that day. I wanted to get to know you better. You're smart and sharp and good at your job. You—interest me, Michelle."

"Oh, and most women don't?" she asked snidely.

"Only physically. With you—it's more."

"Yes, of course. You admire my brains *and* my body," Michelle said, scoffing. "Come on, Steve. Reel it in. I'm not biting."

"It's not a line, Michelle." He sounded hurt. So genuinely wounded that she reflexively turned to him to see if he really was.

With one deft but leisurely move, Steve closed the small gap between them, slipping one arm around her shoulders and tilting her chin upward with his other hand. "Not even a little nibble?" He smiled at her, his eyes warm and filled with humor.

To her dismay, Michelle found herself responding to his roguishly teasing smile with a hesitant smile of her own. What she ought to be was annoyed with him, she reminded herself. He'd been toying with her. Hadn't he? Perhaps she should be furious with him.

But she couldn't seem to work up the righteous anger required. And now he was so very close, his arm around her, his sensual smiling mouth heart-stoppingly near to hers. His long fingers slipped from her chin to her neck to caress the sensitive skin which tingled under his fingertips, sending ripples of fire deep to the very core of her.

"How do you do it?" she asked shakily. She could feel the heat emanating from his body. The musky male odor of soap and after-shave and something *indefinably him* sent her senses swimming.

"Do what?" The husky timbre of his voice was as powerfully seductive as his eyes that had turned heavy and hungry and slumberous with desire.

With his one arm around her and the other stroking her neck, Michelle felt surrounded by the warm, male strength of him. She was vaguely aware that she ought to push him away but she pushed the thought away instead and sat still, gazing into his eyes like one mesmerized. "You know," she murmured tremulously. "Turn things around this way. We were arguing and then suddenly—"

Her voice trailed off as he touched his lips to hers, so lightly and gently she almost thought she'd imagined it. "We were arguing to keep ourselves from doing this," he said in a voice so smoky and intimate and sexually stimulating that a tremor of longing rocked her. Her eyelids dropped closed.

Steve's movements were slow and assured as he drew her back against the cushions. He cupped her cheek with his palm, his fingers moving rhythmically, erotically, as he brushed her lips with his once more. "Sitting there in that restaurant tonight," he breathed the words softly, seductively, as his mouth continued its languid, confident caresses of her lips, her cheeks, the curve of her jaw. "I wanted to touch you so much."

His hand, which had been resting on her shoulder, slid down her back and began to knead the hollow of her waist. He spread his fingers to span the flatness of her belly to the underside of her breast. Michelle felt a dizzying heat erupt within her. The tips of his fingers seemed to be sending sparks of electricity to her every nerve ending. Reflexively she crossed her legs and leaned closer to him, mindlessly seeking the source of that heady male warmth.

With amazing dexterity, Steve's hands moved and shifted so that one was stroking the silky length of her thigh, exposed as her short skirt skimmed higher, while his other hand captured her nape, holding her to receive the full, firm descent of his mouth.

Michelle waited achingly as shudders of desire chased along her spine. She had never been aroused so swiftly, so hotly. Dazed and yearning, she did not think to credit his expert technique for the wild sensations leaping to life within her. She believed them to be a result of her own emotions, her feelings for him, feelings she'd been fighting all evening. Now, in his arms, every ardent, expectant part of her gave up the fight.

"I've been wanting to taste you," Steve murmured huskily as he finally, masterfully, took possession of her mouth.

Her lips opened under his as her arms slid slowly around his neck. His tongue slipped into her mouth to explore the inner softness and Michelle clung to him, drowning in the kiss that grew deeper and hungrier. Still, she ached for an even deeper closeness. There was a rightness in the way he held her, a rightness in the way they were kissing. It was as if she had been waiting her whole life for him and for this sweet, burgeoning passion that flared between them.

Her body arched into his hands and she whispered his name. A deep, primal growl rumbled in Steve's throat, a mating sound, one that he could not control. It shook him, that sudden explosive loss of control. His breathing was fast and shallow and his entire body ached and throbbed with intense sexual need. He'd never gotten so excited so fast— and simply from kissing, too.

What had started as a light, playful experimental kiss, begun more to satisfy a certain curiosity than compelled by a driving force, had swiftly, irrevocably turned into something else entirely. Something beyond his ken, beyond his control.

He felt like a match striking tinder, his body igniting into flames as Michelle first yielded to his kiss, then became an active participant, kissing him back with an ardor that sent wildfire ripping through him. When she clung to him and moved sinuously, sensuously against him, her sweet mouth open and hungry under his, a hot fierce pressure built and grew explosively inside him.

Unable to hold back, he slid one big hand down the wide neckline of her dress. He encountered the silk and lace of her bra but did not let that impede him. His fingers slipped inside to cup her bare breast beneath the material. He caressed the rounded softness, drawing breathless little gasps from her.

Michelle's eyes were tightly closed and she moaned softly as he rubbed her nipples into taut buds of fire. She twisted restlessly, trembling at the wild sensations his touch aroused. It felt so good; she didn't want him to stop. When he withdrew his hand, she whimpered in protest.

"Easy, baby," Steve soothed, his voice deep and rasping. "Let's get you out of this." He smoothed his hands over her back, looking for a zipper or buttons and finding neither. Frustration seared him. "How do you get this thing off?"

He tugged at the stretchy fabric of the dress. She must've pulled it on over her head—or stepped into it, working it up and over her torso. Steve groaned. Either way, removing it was not going to be easy.

That same revelation jarred Michelle out of the sensual mists that had enveloped her. This was an enticing, sexy dress, but it was one that required privacy to take on and off. The contortions, tugging and wiggling involved in doing so were neither enticing nor sexy for a lover to observe.

Lover! The word bounced around her head like a ricocheting bullet. As she emerged from under the spell of his powerful virility, full awareness of what she'd done—and what she'd been about to do!—assailed Michelle with devastating force. Her body turned from pliant to rigid as she tried to wrench away from his grasp.

"Let me go!" She took great gulping breaths of air while her shocked eyes locked into combat with the velvety depths of his.

Steve moved a few inches away, but did not release her. His whole body was one throbbing, burning ache. "Michelle," he began hoarsely.

"No!" She pushed at his chest, hard. Her unexpected strength caught him off guard long enough for her to break free. She jumped to her feet. "I can't believe it!" Outrage at herself, at him and at the overwhelming sexual chemistry between them, fueled her already volatile reaction. "You're as slick as an oil spill! You made me feel comfortable and—safe—with you. You tricked me into relaxing my guard around you. You said you didn't need a woman's capitulation, that I wouldn't have to fight you off but—"

"There was no need for you to fight," Steve reminded her, an odd expression on his face. "You were with me all the way, baby." He wanted to pull her back in his arms, to crush her down onto the sofa and kiss her into hot and hungry submission. Would she let him?

"You arrogant, egotistical, despicable liar!" Michelle raged.

Steve winced. Obviously she would not. "I'm not a liar," he said tightly. "A good lobbyist loses his credibility if he lies and loss of credibility means loss of access. I am not a liar, Michelle," he repeated.

"I'm not talking about lobbying, you snake. I'm talking about what you told me tonight. All that reassurance about not making a pass and then you did just that." And had achieved devastating success with it, too! Michelle seethed.

"I *said* I'd never force a woman," said Steve. His own temper was beginning to rise, despite his attempts to contain it. She could get to him like no one else. "And I didn't force you into anything, Michelle. Anyway, it's not like I seduced you. We were only kissing!"

Only kissing! She felt as if he'd slapped her in the face. *Only kissing?* That's how he regarded it, that's all it meant to him—only a kiss. Another woman, another kiss, another weekend. Michelle remembered the passion that had flared between them, the pleasure, that fierce sense of rightness, of having found something unique and special that could not be duplicated with anyone else. Clearly he had experienced something else entirely. Her face burned with the shame of decimated pride.

"*Only kissing,* you say?" She would never, ever let him know how deeply she'd been wounded by that trite dismissal. Instead Michelle tore into him like a virago. "You seem to have forgotten that you had your hand down the front of my dress!"

"And you loved it!" Steve growled. She'd asked for that, he assured himself. When she drew back her hand and slapped his cheek, he silently admitted that he had asked for that, too.

Michelle stared at the reddening handprint on his cheek with fascinated horror. "I've never hit anyone before in my life," she murmured.

"There's a first time for everything." Steve gingerly touched his cheek. "I can't say I'm thrilled to be the first guy you decked."

Michelle gulped. "You—you deserved it!"

"Did I?"

"Yes! Because nothing means anything to you! You have different women in different cities on different weekends but essentially, it's all the same because if your partners are interchangeable and replaceable, then nothing that happens with one of them is of any importance. Everything and everyone is the same to you."

Steve shifted uncomfortably. His sister Jamie had said much the same thing to him too many times to count, but hearing it from Michelle was somehow more disturbing.

"Well, if it's any consolation to you, this date is definitely different from any other I've ever had," he said defensively. "And you're certainly nothing like any other woman I've ever gone out with. You patronized me all through dinner, you made it very clear that nothing less than a lethal blizzard could ever gain me entry to your apartment, you quarreled with me, insulted me and slugged me. You can believe me when I say that this evening—and you—stand apart from any other."

Michelle folded her arms in front of her chest and glowered at him. "Good!"

He met her smoldering glare with one of his own. *"Good?"*

"Yes! I'd rather be the most miserable date you've ever had than an indistinguishable and forgotten face in your crowd of admirers!"

And while he was mulling over how to reply to that, every light in the apartment simultaneously went out, plunging them into total darkness.

Four

Michelle gasped. Steve cursed. They waited for a few seconds for the lights to flicker back on. Nothing happened.

"Do you think the power lines are down?" Michelle asked anxiously.

"Could be. Listen to that wind howling."

Steve's voice came as a disembodied sound in the darkness, but Michelle was inordinately relieved to hear it. There was something frightening about being plunged into this impenetrable blackness and something reassuring to know that she wasn't alone. Even if the other person there did happen to be Steve-The-Snake-Saraceni.

And then it struck her. "If there is no electricity, there won't be any heat."

"I'm sure it'll be on again soon," Steve said soothingly, wishing he believed it. It was windy and freezing, the roads were impassable, and the chances of a line crew going out to work on downed power lines seemed slim to none.

Another minute passed in dark silence. Neither Michelle nor Steve moved. The only sound was the eerie, lonely wail of the wind.

"What if the electricity doesn't come on soon?" Michelle mused aloud. "This building isn't well insulated at all. The place loses so much heat . . ."

Her voice trailed off. There was no use stating the obvious. That without continuing electrical heat to replace that which was lost through the too thin walls and windows and assorted cracks and crevices, the temperature in the apartment would drop quickly.

"Relax. The power will be restored momentarily." Steve sounded even less convinced than the last time he'd offered assurance. "In the meantime, we could light some candles. You do have candles, I hope?"

"I wish I did but I don't," Michelle said glumly. "I never thought to buy any. I'm sorry."

"Don't apologize. If we were at my place, we'd be out of luck, too. I don't have candles, either. You do have a flashlight, of course?"

Michelle bit her lip, feeling inadequate indeed. "No, I don't."

"I bet you don't have any tools, either. Not even the basics—hammer, nails, wrench, pliers."

"I keep meaning to buy all that stuff," Michelle said defensively. "But I'm never in a hardware store and—"

"As the son of a master carpenter, I'm appalled. I bought those basic tools before I even bought furniture for my place. Sort of a Saraceni legacy, I guess. Well, all isn't lost, we do have another option. I'll go door to door and ask your neighbors for candles or a flashlight."

He groped his way, slowly and carefully to the door, called goodbye to her and was gone. Being familiar with the layout of the room, Michelle quickly found the door and waited by it, peering out into the hall through a crack. She could see nothing but complete darkness. Even the street-light at the end of the block was out.

Steve returned a short time later, shining a flashlight. "I got one candle." He pressed a small, short one into her hand. "And the guy in 2E is letting me borrow this flashlight long enough to go down to my car and get my things."

"Your things?" she echoed.

"My gym bag. I keep it in my car. I have a sweat suit and wool socks in there—all clean—so I can put them on. I'm not about to sleep in my new sport coat and anyway, without heat, I'll need something warmer."

Michelle allowed herself to breathe again. "Yes, of course."

Steve shone the light upon her face. "What did you think, that I'd packed some overnight gear with the full expectation of sleeping over with you tonight?" He didn't give her time to answer. "You did! The expression on your face tells it all."

"Stop wasting the batteries by shining that thing at me," Michelle grumbled.

"You see, you were wrong about me." Steve sounded extraordinarily pleased. "I simply planned to take you to dinner, not to bed. I hope this proves to you that I'm not the indiscriminate, compulsive womanizer you've accused me of being."

"As if you care what I think of you," Michelle said wryly.

"Strangely enough, I do." He no longer sounded pleased, he sounded confused. He beat a hasty retreat. "I'll just grab my coat and head on out to my car. You are going to let me back in, aren't you?"

"I don't have much choice," Michelle replied ungraciously. She wasn't about to make the mistake of believing that her opinion of him actually mattered to him. After all, this was a man whose little black book had multi-state listings.

Alone now in the apartment, Michelle used a small juice glass on a plate to improvise a holder for the candle and lit it. The flame was small but so bright in the pitch blackness that it seemed to cast a great glow throughout the room. She saw Burton the cat still asleep on the sofa. He'd remained oblivious to the prior goings-on there, except to curl himself into a ball.

Her cheeks flushed at the memory of those tempestuous moments. The way Steve had made her feel . . . the throbbing excitement, the delicious sense of spinning out of control. When she felt a tingling, tightening ache deep in the core of her, Michelle banished those heady reminiscences. They were too potent; she didn't dare allow herself to indulge in them. She must always keep in mind that Steve Saraceni had undoubtedly made hosts of other women feel incredibly, excitingly sexy, too.

Flustered, she hurried into her bedroom, the small candle lighting her way. For the first time she noticed that the double bed seemed to dominate—indeed, fill—the small room. The branches of a tree limb rattled against the windows and Michelle jumped with a startled gasp. She couldn't remember ever being this nervous and on edge.

The room was already getting chilly. In an effort to keep her bills down, she never set her thermostat very high anyway, and the cessation of heat combined with the fierce wind outside were making their effects felt. In a very short while, the apartment was going to be uncomfortably cold.

A quick glance at her watch revealed that it was past midnight. As there was no electricity, the sensible thing to do was to go to bed and sleep through the rest of the storm. *But how could she ever sleep with Steve here?* How could she even get ready for bed—undress!—with him in the apartment?

That unnerving scenario galvanized Michelle into taking advantage of Steve's temporary absence. She undressed quickly, tossing her discarded clothes into the closet. It was a most uncharacteristic action. Having grown up in crowded quarters, shuttled between her parents, she'd become meticulous about putting everything in its place. A way to exert some control over uncontrollable circumstances, perhaps. Or maybe she'd simply been born with a gene for neatness.

But there was no time to be neat tonight, not when Steve's return was imminent. The chill in the air made her shiver, and it was only going to get colder. Michelle swiftly donned a full set of thermal long underwear and pulled on a dark blue sweat suit on top of those. She had just put on her second pair of socks when Steve pounded at the door.

Carrying the candle, she hurried to let him in. He was covered with snow. "You're a dead ringer for Nanook of the North," Michelle observed.

"Ah, a little blizzard humor. What's next? An Abominable Snowman joke?" He flicked a glob of snow at her and she squealed and jumped away. "I turned on the car radio while I was out there. The big story is the weather, of course."

Steve removed his overcoat and brushed the snow from it, then kicked off his wet shoes, talking all the while. "They have no idea when it'll stop snowing, the winds are gusting up to forty miles an hour and half the city is without power. The turnpike's closed and there's been a twenty-one-car pileup on I-81."

"That's awful!" Michelle exclaimed.

"Yeah. They've dispatched all snow removal equipment to the accident site to allow emergency vehicles to get the injured to the hospitals. Forget getting the power restored until sometime tomorrow, at the very earliest."

Michelle watched, wide-eyed, as Steve shrugged out of his sport coat. When he took off his tie and began to unbutton his shirt, she sprang to action. "You can use the bathroom first." She shoved the candle plate in his hand. "While you're getting un—uh, getting dressed, I'll get the sheets for the sofa.''

"And plenty of blankets. It's already getting cold in here. By morning, it'll really be—what's the matter?" He stared at Michelle, who had just heaved a dispirited groan.

"I don't have any blankets," she said.

"What?''

"I've never needed extra blankets," she explained, her tone both defensive and apologetic. "I have a goose-down comforter for my bed. It's one of those that's guaranteed for arctic temperatures, and it's all I need. I have a ribcord cotton spread that I use in warmer weather.'' She lowered her eyes. "You can use it tonight. If you wear your coat—''

"Forget it, Michelle. My coat is wet from the snow and it's only a thin wool, not all that warm anyway. And a lightweight cotton spread is useless on a night like this, particularly when there's no heat! You and I are going to share—the bed, the arctic quilt, and our body heat. It's the only way.''

"No way," she cried. Her heartbeat had doubled, tripled its rate. "If you think I'm going to bed with you, you're—''

"You can't seriously believe that I'm making a play for you now?" Steve interrupted incredulously. "Baby, you've taken paranoia to new extremes! I just don't want to freeze to death tonight.'' He snatched his gym bag and stomped into the bathroom, leaving Michelle alone in the darkness.

What was she going to do now? Her lungs felt full to bursting and a breathless weakness assailed her. *She couldn't spend the night in the same bed with Steve!* The mere thought of having him in her apartment, carefully installed in the other room while she slept, had been unnerving enough, but this—

"Your turn." The sound of Steve's silky voice echoed as the bathroom door opened a short while later. The shadowy glow of the candle signaled his appearance.

"I will absolutely, categorically, not allow this to happen," Michelle said emphatically.

She turned around to watch him approaching her. He was wearing baggy gray sweatpants and an equally roomy gray sweatshirt with heavy gray socks on his feet. And he looked as devastatingly handsome as he had in his dress clothes, maybe even better, for the loose casual clothes emphasized his hard, muscular virility in a way that the designer duds did not.

Michelle's mouth was suddenly dry. Her voice lost its assertiveness and became pleading. "Steve, surely you realize that we can't—"

"I realize that we have no choice in this, Michelle," he cut in briskly. "You've made it very clear that you don't want to share a bed with me, but we're going to. So if you're entertaining any stupid, martyrish notions of sleeping on the sofa yourself with your pathetic cotton spread, you can just forget it. We're going to *sleep,* literally. I'm not using it as a euphemism for making love. We're both adults and we're both going to act like it. Sensible and practical. *Capiche?*"

Michelle stared at him mutely.

"That's Italian. I'll teach some words to you, if you'd like. You've got all night to learn."

Steve advanced toward her. Michelle automatically backed away.

"Michelle, I'm not going to chase you around the room carrying a candle." His lips quirked wryly. "It's too impractical." He set the candle down on the small end table and headed toward the bedroom. "Good night."

Once again silence reigned in the small apartment. Michelle picked up the candle and glumly trudged into the bathroom. It was always drafty and chilly in the winter, but without any heat coming through the small register, the little room was becoming downright frigid.

She completed her ablutions speedily and hesitantly walked to the threshold of her bedroom. By candlelight she saw her bed and Steve in it, the arctic-proof quilt pulled so high that his black hair was barely visible on the pillow. According to him, she was now supposed to casually climb into bed with him.

She rebelled. Michelle carried the burning candle back into the living room, put on her parka, and sat down on the sofa. It was going to be a very long, very cold night.

She didn't know how long she sat there. The room was steadily growing colder and so was she. Worse, the small candle was melting fast. It would soon burn itself out, leaving her completely in the dark.

"I'm making an exception in your case." Steve was suddenly standing above her. Michelle jumped. She'd been staring out the window at the wind whipping the snow into drifts and hadn't even heard him approach.

Steve scooped her up into his arms before she realized his intentions. "I've never forced a woman to do anything she doesn't want to do, but as the old saying goes, there's a first time for everything."

"Put me down!" Michelle cried. She managed to retain a precarious grip on the precious candle.

"No," Steve gritted. "I'm exhausted but for some perverse reason I can't sleep knowing that you're out here shivering. The only way either of us will get any rest tonight is if I put you in the damn bed and keep you there."

"You can't! I won't!" cried Michelle, wriggling fiercely in his arms.

A wolflike growl rumbled in Steve's throat. "You are without a doubt the most stubborn, the most obstinate, the most unreasonable woman I've ever met." He started into the bedroom at the same moment that Michelle dropped the plate with the candle. It landed with a thud on the carpet, the flame snuffed out on its way to the floor.

"See what you made me do!" she cried. "Now we have no light at all."

"It doesn't matter, we don't need it. We'll both be in bed for the rest of the night."

Steve carried her into the bedroom, slowly finding his way in the darkness. Michelle stopped fighting. The thought of being dropped to the floor, like the candle, effectively quelled her efforts. She clutched at his sweatshirt, feeling dizzily disoriented in the pitch blackness.

Steve dumped her onto the bed. Swift as a cat pouncing on its hapless prey, he had her under the quilt and pinned with his arms and legs. "I'll let you go if you promise to stay put, Michelle."

Michelle blinked. It was so dark in the room that it didn't matter if her eyes were open or shut. The bed was very warm and her head sank into the softness of the pillows.

"Michelle, I swear you have nothing to fear from me," Steve murmured softly, coaxingly. "Think about it. Logistically, even if I were in the throes of flaming lust, I couldn't do much about it. Neither of us are exactly dressed for a passionate hop in the sack—or undressed as the case may be."

He did have a point. And as she lay quietly, Michelle was suddenly, wearily aware of how tired she was. She had no energy left to keep fighting Steve, and the thought of the cold living room was appalling.

"All right," she whispered. "I'll stay. But let go of me." He was holding her tight and the hard male strength of him was wreaking havoc with her senses. If he didn't release her soon, she feared she might end up begging him not to.

Steve slowly unwound his arms and legs from around her and stretched out beside her, flat on his back. Michelle rolled onto her side, as close to the edge of the bed as she could get without falling out. They lay in silence for several long dark moments.

"Michelle, would you mind if I asked you a personal question?" Steve's voice was deep and low and unexpectedly urgent.

"You can ask, but I might not answer it," she replied warily.

"Have you ever been raped?"

"What?" She gasped. "No!" Michelle rolled to her other side to face him but she couldn't see him or anything else, only the enveloping intimacy of darkness. "Why did you ask me that?"

"Your reaction to having me spend the night with you was—extreme, to say the least. I thought maybe it wasn't me personally you objected to, but the idea of having a man, any man, here. If you'd been badly traumatized by one, well, that would explain a lot."

"It's inconceivable to you that I prefer my privacy?" she flared. "You find it easier to assume that I'm a victim of a violent crime than to accept the fact that I don't eagerly welcome a man into my bed on our *first date?* A man, I might add, who has made it quite clear that he's allergic to commitment, a man who has spent too many nights in too many different beds with—"

"Touché," Steve interrupted dryly. "But we've already covered all that, Michelle. Let's not repeat ourselves."

She rolled over to her other side again, making no reply.

"Michelle?"

She heaved an impatient sigh. "Yes?"

"I'm glad you weren't raped," he said huskily. "I can't stand the thought of you being hurt that way. Believe it or not, I'd rather you have a relentless aversion to me than to have suffered through—that."

The warmth that stole through her had nothing to do with the arctic-proof quilt. "I don't have an aversion to you," she confessed quietly. "It's just—I—I guess I'm not used to sharing a bed. Not for the past several years, anyway. When I was a kid visiting my dad, I used to share my stepsister Courtney's bed and when my stepfather's daughter Lisa visited him, she slept in my bed with me. But since I've grown up and been on my own, I—"

"Haven't you ever, uh, shared a bed with anyone else?" Steve interrupted curiously. "I'm not talking stepsisters here, I mean, well—" He paused, took a breath and plunged ahead. "Guys. You know, boyfriends, lovers." It was, he realized, the first time he'd ever quizzed a woman on her past. He'd never been interested enough to even speculate about any other woman's past.

"Guys, boyfriends, lovers?" Michelle repeated in tones as frozen as the current temperature outdoors. "You're asking me if I've slept around with a lot of men?"

"No, no, of course not!" Steve interjected quickly. He was aghast. It was unlike him to commit such a blatant faux pas. "I, uh, was just—" There was no way to salvage this, he acknowledged. It was time to divert the issue entirely "How many people are in your family anyway?" he asked abruptly. "You've mentioned sisters, brothers, parents and steps—I can't keep track of them all."

Had there been any light, he would've seen Michelle roll her eyes heavenward. But she was more than willing to drop the subject of all those guys, boyfriends and lovers he assumed she'd entertained in her bed. Telling a bedroom Olympian like Steve Saraceni that her experiences in bed-sharing included only her stepsisters and her cat would be extremely humiliating. And far too revealing.

Michelle accepted his conversational olive branch. "My family is a tangle of wholes, steps and halves," she murmured. "I have pictures of everybody in the living room I could show you if the lights weren't out. It's much easier to put names with faces."

"I have a fantastic memory for names and titles and who-fits-in-where-with-whom. It's a must in my profession. Test me. Tell me the names of the Careys and their assorted connections and I'll repeat them back to you, one hundred percent correct."

"You've taken on a real challenge," Michelle warned. The unnerving awkwardness was dissipating and she was beginning to relax. Surprisingly, it wasn't so terribly threatening to be lying there talking with him. It was rather cozy.

"We'll start with Cathy, Warren and Hayden, my full sister and brothers," she said. "They're in their thirties and married with children now. They were all in school by the time I came along."

"You were a surprise, huh?"

"No, I was an unforeseen, unplanned for, unwanted accident," Michelle replied matter-of-factly. "Mom and Dad were planning to separate. They'd been to the lawyers and had the papers drawn up and then my mother—"

"—Found out she was pregnant with you," Steve concluded. "Whew! Talk about being caught in a trap!" Then he realized he was talking to the full-grown version of that "trap." He cleared his throat. "I mean, I'm sure they were delighted. You offered them a second chance at happiness."

"My appearance prolonged their marriage for two more miserable years," Michelle amended. "But they were finally divorced and two years later Daddy married Kate, who was a widow with three children, Mark, Ashlinn and Courtney. I liked them from the very beginning. Sometimes Courtney and I would pretend we were twins since we were the same age."

"Imagine marrying a woman with *three children!*" marveled Steve. He couldn't.

"You can't imagine marrying, period," Michelle said dryly.

"We're not talking about me. You're supposed to be giving me a sweeping overview of the Carey much-extended family, remember?"

"If you insist. My mother married Tim Lowell, who was divorced with two kids of his own, Lonnie and Lisa. They lived with their mother but visited their dad twice a month and two weeks in the summer. When I was eight, Mom and Tim had the twins, Debbie and Donna, my half sisters."

"A real 'yours, mine and ours' family," Steve remarked. He proceeded to correctly recite all the names and tangled relationships back to her. "Why didn't your dad and the widow Kate have a baby together? Seems like having children is the thing to do in your family."

"They tried. Kate had a couple miscarriages. It just wasn't meant to be."

"Bet you were glad," Steve said bluntly. "Seems to me there were way too many kids floating around Carey and Company."

"You just hit on my most shameful childhood secret," Michelle said wryly. As he seemed inherently unshockable, she found it surprisingly easy to confide in him. "I desperately did not want Dad and Kate to have a baby. I suppose I was threatened by the thought of yet another child. I always felt lost in the shuffle while I was growing up. I knew I wasn't particularly special in either home. I was one among many and I didn't stand out in any way."

Fungible. Interchangeable. Not unique or special. The words echoed in Steve's head. They were Michelle's own words, describing his attitude toward women. He abruptly sat up in bed. She'd felt that way as a little girl, as a child among too many other kids. No wonder viewing herself as a woman among too many other women rankled her so. He remembered what she'd said about preferring to be his worst date instead of just another indistinguishable one. Suddenly her previously incomprehensible statement made sense to him.

Steve was both astonished and a bit proud of the connection he'd made. He was actually beginning to understand Michelle! It was a first for him. If he'd had a dime for every time the charge of "you just don't understand" had been hurled at him, he could retire as a wealthy man tomorrow.

"What's the matter?" Michelle asked worriedly, sitting up in bed.

Steve realized that he'd bolted upright and remained that way. "Uh, nothing. Just a cramp." He laid back down. "Leg cramp," he improvised. "I get them sometimes."

"Do you want some aspirin?" she asked concernedly.

"No, no, I'm fine now. Lie down, it's okay."

Michelle laid back down and snuggled into the goose-down thickness. "I almost forgot to compliment you on your excellent memory," she said softly. "It takes my friends a long time to get everybody in my family straight and some never do." She chuckled. "Ed gets so confused he—"

"Ed?" Steve interrupted. He tried and failed to identify the peculiar searing sensation tearing through him.

"Ed Dineen. You know, the state senator. My boss."

He could hear the smile in her voice as she talked on and on about Ed Dineen. Ed was brilliant, honorable, and conscientious. Scrupulously honest and loyal. Witty, perceptive and sensitive. A wonderful public speaker.

Steve shifted restlessly in the bed. He'd never been jealous of anyone or anything in his entire life. There was no need, not with his towering self-confidence and unbroken chain of successes. But lying here listening to Michelle rave on about another man, he identified the choking, bitter feeling ripping through him as jealousy.

"Dineen's married, isn't he?" Steve asked sourly.

"Oh, yes," Michelle said, still bubbling with enthusiasm. "His wife, Valerie, is just wonderful. And they have two adorable children, Teddy and Danielle. Valerie and Ed both went to Penn State, you know. That's where they met. Ed was on the basketball team there. He's still a rabid college basketball fan."

Her enthusiastic endorsement of Valerie and the children helped a little. But Steve had known too many women in the political arena who devoted their lives to their bosses, living vicariously through them, viewing them through worshipful eyes. Even if those relationships weren't sexual, the attachment was just as powerful. Maybe more so. As he well knew, sex could be conveniently distancing, but adoration was definitely personal.

"Sounds like your—*job*—is very important to you," he said stiffly.

"Oh, yes, I love my work. It's the most important thing in my life," Michelle affirmed earnestly. "I'm fascinated with the way government works, the legislative process, the inner workings of the political system. Aren't you?"

"Well, yes," Steve admitted grudgingly.

"Being part of it means being able to make a difference. Every day is interesting, every day I learn something new and meet new people."

"That's certainly true." Steve forgot his fit of pique as they talked politics, trading views and opinions late into the night.

It was a night of firsts for them both. The first time that Steve had ever spent a platonic night in a woman's bed, the first time that Michelle had ever allowed a man to share her bed. When they finally fell asleep, it was nearly dawn.

They awakened late in the morning, with the cat snuggled under the covers between them. The power was still off and the apartment was bone-jarringly cold. Unlike a blizzard-proof dogsled, Steve's car remained mired in the snowy terrains of the parking lot.

There was nothing for Michelle and Steve to do but to climb back into bed with the sandwiches they'd made and talk some more. They spent the entire day there, snacking and talking. It was amazing how much they had to say to each other and how easily it was to say it. Nothing seemed too trivial to reveal.

"Everybody claims to love those old movies from the thirties, those screwball comedies and dark melodramas. So I pretend that I do, too," Steve confided. "But to be perfectly honest, I don't get their appeal. I like the movies of today—with lots of action and car chases and special effects."

"I have an equally shameful confession," Michelle offered. "Remember the outrage when those old black and white movie classics were colorized for TV? Well, I like them better in color."

"So do I." Steve grinned. "I guess it's a good thing we chose careers based in Harrisburg, not Hollywood, hmm?"

"For our own sakes as well as the sake of the film industry," added Michelle.

They exchanged congenial, confidential smiles.

It was almost nine o'clock that night when the power was finally restored. At the same moment that a rush of heat came blasting through the vents, every light in the living room flashed on. Michelle and Steve were huddled under the quilt in the bedroom.

"The power's back on!" she exclaimed. Part of her was relieved. It was extremely difficult to do without electricity in an all-electric apartment. But another part of her felt a twinge of regret. The power outage had given her the opportunity to spend time with Steve, to get to know him in a way she otherwise never would have. And that was over now.

"Three cheers for Med Ed." But despite his endorsement of the electric company, Steve made no move to leave the bed.

Michelle switched on the bedside lamp before slipping out of the bed. She caught a glimpse of herself in the mirror and was horrified at the sight of her rumpled sweat suit, her tousled hair and flushed face, totally devoid of makeup. It didn't matter that she'd spent the entire day with Steve without an ounce of concern about her appearance. Now a self-conscious wave swept over her and she felt like turning off the lights before he could get a good look at her.

The return of civilization, it seemed, changed everything.

Steve sensed her withdrawal. He wondered if he could persuade her to let him spend another night here, in bed with her. This time with heat. And minus three layers of clothes. Tonight, *no* clothes would be required.

Michelle turned at that moment to see his unmistakably predatory smile. He reminded her of Burton stalking the new parakeet she'd brought home one day from the mall pet shop. Watching, assessing, planning. Waiting for the chance to make his move. She'd taken the little bird back to the store, knowing it was unsafe here. Now it appeared that she was in the same predicament.

"We should see if your car is still stuck in the lot," she said with sudden brisk efficiency. She was pulling on her outdoor gear before Steve sat up in bed.

He finally did so with a resigned sigh. "You don't have to go outside, Michelle. I'll check on it." Naturally he would discover his car still hopelessly stuck, he promised himself.

Michelle met his eyes. And correctly interpreted the gleam she saw there. "I'll be glad to go with you," she insisted firmly.

They trudged out together to find that the building superintendent had already arranged for the lot to be plowed and salted. With the reliability of a dogsled in the Arctic, Steve's car glided smoothly out of its space. He was free. There was no excuse not to collect his things and go home.

Michelle walked him to the door. They lingered there for a few moments, he as reluctant to leave as she was to see him go.

"I could stay tonight," Steve said, gazing intently at her. He made no effort to hide the desire and determination in his eyes.

"On the sofa, in the living room, with the cotton spread?" Michelle asked lightly. It couldn't be any other way. If she let him make love to her, he would add her name to his scorecard and forget her. And as much as she'd enjoyed being with him, she was too much of a realist to believe that a romantic night in bed with her would alter his views on freedom and commitment. He'd said it himself— he wasn't looking for love, he just wanted to have a good time.

Steve shook his head, still smiling that smooth unfathomable smile of his. "Sorry, honey. I'm too old for pajama parties," he said, a bit regretfully. "With me, it's all the way or nothing."

Michelle nodded. "I know."

"Hey, we did have fun though, didn't we?" He took both her hands in his. "You're a good sport, Michelle." She really was, he acknowledged thoughtfully. She hadn't whined or complained or sulked about the discomfort and inconvenience. "If I'm ever in another power outage, I hope it'll be with you."

Her eyes suddenly, unexpectedly welled with tears. "Me, too," she said huskily, lowering her head to avert her gaze.

Steve dropped a quick kiss on the top of her head, murmured goodbye, and was gone. It really couldn't be any other way, he told himself as he drove home. He liked Michelle; she was a great girl, but she really wasn't his type. She was too bright, sweet, funny, warm, loyal, sexy and interesting....

He shook his head. He was becoming depressed. It was definitely time to put another spin on the situation. So he started over. Michelle really wasn't his type. She was too clever, driven, rigid, uptight, bossy, intractable. And she was too family centered, despite her dedication to her career. He didn't doubt for a minute that she wanted far more than he was prepared to give—like a ring, a baby, a house in the suburbs.

Images of growing up in Merlton with his ever-loving smothering family tumbled through his head, along with the voices of his parents and sisters and grandmother. *Stevie, don't go, you could get hurt. Stevie, don't do that, it could be dangerous. Stevie, play with me, come with me, take me with you. Stevie, that's too expensive, save your money. Stevie, when are you going to settle down with a nice girl? Your life doesn't really begin until you're married.*

Those restless, suffocating feelings that had driven him out of Merlton resurfaced yet again. He wasn't ready for the restrictive claustrophobia of family life, not yet! A night in Michelle Carey's bed was *not* worth the marital life sentence it would cost him!

Five

"**T**he turn out tonight is fantastic," Michelle remarked as she and the other Dineen staffers surveyed the well-dressed crowd packed into the Waterworks, the restored old building along the shore of the Susquehanna River. The Dineens had rented the place for tonight's party.

"Confidentially, I thought it was a bit sappy when Valerie picked Valentine's Day to announce Ed's plans to run for re-election," said Leigh Wilson. "And when she suggested kicking off the campaign with a Valentine's Day party fund-raiser, I cringed. Sending out invitations pasted on red cut-out hearts strikes me as excessively cornball."

"Well, everyone who was invited is here," Michelle said with satisfaction.

"At five hundred dollars a plate, it's a nice boost to Ed's war chest," added Claire Collins.

Leigh frowned. "I do wish Valerie had shown a little restraint with the decorations. There must be a billion candy hearts hanging on those mobiles dangling from the ceiling. Everybody has been commenting on them. It's embarrassing."

"Valerie is very creative," Michelle said loyally. "And I've heard nothing but compliments on those candy heart mobiles."

"Valerie Dineen could string dog biscuits and hang them from the ceiling and you'd approve, Michelle." Leigh sighed exasperatedly. "You think everything she does is wonderful. If you'd be a little more objective you would see that she holds Ed back in many ways. She turns down almost all speaking invitations because she's so bad at giving speeches, she still hasn't lost all the weight she gained with the last baby and—"

"She's Ed's wife," Michelle cut in sharply. "She's kind and shy and he adores her. If you'll excuse me, I see someone I want to say hello to."

She didn't, but she did want to get away from Leigh. Michelle crossed the room, disturbed by the other woman's open, vitriolic criticism of sweet Valerie Dineen. She was so preoccupied that she didn't see the dark-suited figure step in front of her until she almost crashed headlong into him.

"Whoa! Where's the fire?" Steve Saraceni asked jocularly.

"Oh, I'm terribly sorry. I'm afraid I wasn't looking where I was going." Michelle was proud of the smooth steadiness of her voice and the impersonal pleasantry of her smile. Steve Saraceni would never know that her heart had leapt into her throat at the sight of him and her stomach was still doing flips.

She was annoyed by her acute reaction to him. It had been three weeks since the blizzard had forced them to hole up in her apartment and she hadn't heard a word from him since. Not that she'd expected to, Michelle continually reminded herself. Yet for days after the storm she'd waited in a state of heightened anticipation for him to call. When he did not, an aching disappointment nagged at her. That, too, had worn off as she'd accepted what she should have realized from the very beginning. The wintry weekend of conversation and closeness meant nothing to Steve. He'd undoubtedly forgotten it—and her—as soon as he'd left her apartment.

She moved to pass him, but he stepped to the side, blocking her way. "You look great tonight, Michelle," he said, his dark eyes sparkling with admiration. "Red is definitely your color."

"Valerie Dineen asked all the staff to wear some shade of red in keeping with the Valentine's Day theme of the party," Michelle said coolly. She'd had to buy her strawberry-red knit sweater and matching pleated skirt because she had never owned anything red. She'd always considered the color too bright for her tastes.

"I was pleased to receive an invitation to the party tonight," said Steve, sounding credibly sincere. "I like Ed Dineen and Legislative Engineers was delighted to contribute to his campaign."

As a member of the senator's staff, Michelle said what she would say to any contributor. "I'm sure Senator Dineen appreciates your support."

Steve smiled. "Ed's a great guy. I met him a couple of weeks ago and we've had lunch together."

"Yes, I know. Ed was terribly pleased when you recognized him as a Penn State basketball star," Michelle said dryly. She was certain that the "accidental" meeting on the Capitol stairs between Steve and Ed Dineen had been premeditated and carefully arranged on Steve's part.

But she'd been disturbed to learn that Steve had made use of the information about Ed's college basketball career, facts she had provided during their weekend together. Being Steve, he'd used them well, to gain access to the senator. Now, having been subjected to the full force of the

Saraceni charm, Ed Dineen was quite favorably disposed to the lobbyist.

Perhaps she was being too sensitive but Michelle felt somewhat used. She was undecided as to whether Steve Saraceni's operating methods were sneaky and underhanded or deft and skillful. She couldn't trust her own judgment where he was concerned and *that* concerned her.

Michelle glanced purposefully at her watch. "I've got to run. It was so nice seeing you again." Her tone and expression were blatantly insincere. She swiftly fled to the cloakroom.

"Leaving so soon?"

Michelle didn't bother to turn around. She knew it was Steve who was suddenly a few steps behind her. And then by her side.

"There's no need for me to stay any longer," she said crisply. "I've put in an appearance here. Ed is busy working the room and my presence isn't required."

"Do you have a date lined up after this?" Steve pressed.

"Of course not," she said incredulously. "It's a Wednesday night." Weekend dates were enough of a rarity for her; weeknight dates were inconceivable.

"It's not such a preposterous question. It is Valentine's Day," Steve reminded her.

"Yes, it is. And naturally, this is a big holiday for you, isn't it? I'm sure you singlehandedly boost sales of cards, flowers and candy on this day. After all, you have valentines in four cities."

Steve smiled, his credo being: when in doubt, smile. He also ignored her jibe and laid his hand on her shoulder. "Well, since neither of us have dates tonight, why don't we go somewhere and have a drink together?"

Michelle didn't miss a beat. "No, thank you." She hurried away from him, shoving her coat claim check into the hands of the checker.

Steve followed her, his smile still in place. "Why not?" His voice lowered and turned coaxing. "I thought we were pals, Michelle."

Michelle received her coat and quickly slipped it on, resisting his attempt to help her. "You're mistaken," she said sweetly as she headed to the door. "We're not pals. Good night, Steve."

Steve stared after her. He realized that his jaw was agape and quickly closed his mouth. It was extraordinarily difficult to put his smile back in place. Michelle had given him the brush-off as he'd never received it before.

Back at her apartment, Michelle had just settled down on the couch with Burton purring on her lap when her doorbell sounded. A glance through the peephole revealed a most unexpected sight—Steve Saraceni, holding a big red heart-shaped box that just had to contain chocolates.

Michelle opened the door, laughing. "You've got to be kidding!"

Steve cleared his throat. Laughter, he hadn't expected. "I wanted to give this to you," he said, an uncharacteristic note of uncertainty in his voice. He put the box of candy into her arms.

Michelle looked from it to him. "Do you buy these things wholesale, by the gross? And keep them handily stashed in your car for whenever you run across a prospective valentine?"

Steve grimaced. "I did buy a number of them but not for the reasons you think. I pass out candy to the secretaries and receptionists in the various House and Senate offices every year—it's the only Valentine some of them receive. And you can't accuse me of romancing every secretary in the Capitol. Think how many are married, how many are older. It's business, that's all."

"I see. You give candy to the secretaries and they make it easier for you to get in to see their bosses. Whatever it takes to do the job, hmm?"

The more
you love romance . . .
the more
you'll love this offer

FREE!

Mail this heart today! (See inside)!

**Join us on a Silhouette Honeymoon
and we'll give you
4 Free Books
A Free Victorian Picture Frame
And a Free Mystery Gift**

IT'S A
SILHOUETTE HONEYMOON—
A SWEETHEART OF A FREE OFFER!
HERE'S WHAT YOU GET:

1. Four New Silhouette Desire® Novels—FREE!

Take a Silhouette Honeymoon with four exciting romances—yours FREE from the Silhouette Reader Service™. Each of these hot-off-the-press novels brings you the passion and tenderness of today's greatest love stories…your free passports to bright new worlds of love and foreign adventure.

2. A Lovely Victorian Picture Frame—FREE!

This lovely Victorian pewter-finish miniature is perfect for displaying a treasured photograph. And it's yours FREE as added thanks for giving our Reader Service a try!

3. An Exciting Mystery Bonus—FREE!

With this offer, you'll also receive a special mystery bonus. It is useful as well as practical.

4. Convenient Home Delivery!

Join the Silhouette Reader Service™ and enjoy the convenience of previewing 6 new books every month delivered right to your home. Each book is yours for only $2.49* per book, a saving of 30¢ each off the cover price plus only 69¢ delivery for the entire shipment! If you're not fully satisfied, you can cancel any time, just by sending us a note or shipping statement marked "cancel" or by returning any shipment to us at our cost. Great savings plus convenience add up to a sweetheart of a deal for you!

5. Free Insiders' Newsletter!

You'll get our monthly newsletter packed with news on your favorite writers, upcoming books, even recipes from your favorite authors.

6. More Surprise Gifts!

Because our home subscribers are our most valued readers, when you join the Silhouette Reader Service™, we'll be sending you additional free gifts from time to time—as a token of our appreciation.

START YOUR SILHOUETTE HONEYMOON TODAY—
JUST COMPLETE, DETACH AND MAIL YOUR FREE-OFFER CARD

DETACH AND MAIL TODAY!

PLACE HEART STICKER HERE

GIVE YOUR HEART TO SILHOUETTE

Yes! Please send me my four Silhouette Desire® novels FREE, along with my Free Victorian Picture Frame and Free Mystery Gift. I wish to receive all the benefits of the Silhouette Reader Service™ as explained on the opposite page.

NAME _____
(PLEASE PRINT)

ADDRESS _____ APT. _____

CITY _____

PROVINCE _____ POSTAL CODE _____

326 CIS ADMY
(C-SIL-D-01/92)

SILHOUETTE READER SERVICE "NO-RISK" GUARANTEE

—There's no obligation to buy—and the free gifts remain yours to keep.

—You pay the low subscribers-only discount price and receive books before they appear in stores.

—You may end your subscription any time by sending us a note or shipping statement marked "cancel" or by returning any shipment to us at our cost.

© 1991 HARLEQUIN ENTERPRISES LIMITED

PRINTED IN U.S.A.

DETACH AND MAIL TODAY!

**Business
Reply Mail**

No Postage Stamp
Necessary if Mailed
in Canada

Postage will be paid by

SILHOUETTE READER SERVICE™
P.O. Box 609
Fort Erie, Ontario
L2A 9Z9

Canada Post
Postes Canada
125

"Access is the name of the game," Steve affirmed.

"And you can even write off the cost of all the candy because it's business. Just one question though. How come you gave a heart to me? Does this mean I'm included in your Valentine's Day tax break?"

"That's two questions," Steve corrected silkily. His smile didn't reach his eyes, which were pensive and wary. *What was he doing here?* He had no answer; he'd followed her home impulsively, not allowing himself to think at all, only to act. But he had to admit that giving her the candy had been an inordinately stupid move. Michelle was too bright to be taken in by such a blatant last-minute gesture.

Michelle shrugged. "Well, thanks for the candy." She refused to tell him that it happened to be the only Valentine she'd received. She did not want to be on his access-via-pity list every year. "I'm sure I'll enjoy it." She started to close the door....

Steve wedged his shoulder inside, blocking it open. "Aren't you going to invite me in?"

"Sorry. It's not snowing and the electricity is on tonight."

"And the only way I get invited in is if there's a blizzard raging and the power is out, right?"

"That's right."

He heaved a groan mingled with a sigh. "Ah, Michelle, don't be this way. We had a great time together. Why can't we—"

"—Pick up where we left off?" Michelle inserted with saccharine sweetness. *"Three weeks ago?"*

"It's been that long?" He sounded genuinely surprised. "I've been really busy—went to the Super Bowl one weekend and—"

"Steve, you don't owe me any explanations," she cut in coolly. "In fact, I don't care to hear them. I was simply pointing out that when three weeks pass without a single word, you can't expect to—"

"It's not that I wasn't thinking of you," Steve blurted out.

"Oh, I'm sure you thought about me just as often as I thought about you," Michelle said caustically, pleased with the effects of her tone. She sounded cool and flip, as if the thought of him hadn't crossed her mind once for the past three weeks. She wasn't about to inform him otherwise.

Steve frowned slightly. The truth was that he had thought about her, entirely too much. That had scared him enough into deliberately keeping away from her. Nevertheless he would find himself thinking of her at odd, unguarded moments, wanting to discuss a bit of news with her, to share a joke. It wasn't a good sign. He knew the words to *The Tender Trap*; his father, a Sinatra fan, had played it often enough over the years. What Steve did not want was to find himself living the lyrics.

"Good night, Steve," Michelle said firmly. She would've closed the door to accentuate her point, but didn't as he remained stubbornly wedged in the door frame. There was really no need to bloody him.

He should leave; she clearly wanted him to. Steve had no idea what kept him rooted to the spot, but he didn't budge. "You're the *unfriendliest* woman I've ever known," he accused.

Michelle thought about all those other women he knew, who undoubtedly qualified as ultra friendly—and then some. Her blue eyes flashed. "Coming from you, that's a compliment."

"This is ridiculous!" Steve growled. His cool was definitely beginning to melt. The woman mocked him, quarreled with him, infuriated him. "I don't need this. What am I doing here?"

He was speaking more or less rhetorically but Michelle chose to reply mockingly, "You're trying to pawn off your leftover candy on me in an attempt—a futile one as far as

I'm concerned—to gain access to Ed Dineen. That's what you're doing here.''

Anger surged through him like a burst of adrenaline. ''That's it!'' he spat. He fully intended to stalk out. When it came to the fight-or-flight alternative, he always opted for the convenient ''I'm out of here'' course of action.

But tonight he seemed to be operating under different guidelines. He surprised himself almost as much as her when he caught her arms and yanked her against him. ''You're impossible,'' he snarled. ''You drive me nuts!''

The box of candy slipped from her nerveless fingers and hit the floor. Neither noticed. Their eyes were locked, his dark and fiery, hers startled and wide.

And before Michelle could think, move or breathe, his mouth was opening over hers in a hard, hungry kiss. She struggled, she tried to twist her mouth free, to no avail. Steve kept her pinned firmly against him, his arms wrapped around her as strong as steel bands, his thighs trapping hers, while his mouth plundered her own.

Michelle's mind spun out of control as pleasure exploded within her like a fireball. She wasn't sure when or how, but somewhere along the line she stopped fighting and her emotions took over, responding to the powerful chemistry sizzling between them.

She arched against him, her arms locked around his neck, as he took her mouth deeply over and over again. Her breasts swelled sensuously against the hardness of his chest and she was achingly aware of the burgeoning heat of his thighs pressing into her, tight and hard and close. But not close enough.

Governed by pure instinct, Michelle writhed in his arms, striving to get closer still. A primal feminine need to envelope him and absorb him into her very being surged through her with shattering force.

Their kisses grew longer and hotter and wilder. Michelle's hands roamed over the hard male strength of his back and shoulders. She'd never dreamed there could be so much pleasure in caressing. It was almost as exciting and arousing as being caressed.

Almost. Could there ever be anything as thrilling as the feel of his big hands slipping beneath her sweater to cup the soft fullness of her breasts? His fingers kneaded her sensuously, until her nipples were tautly erect against the lacy fabric of her brassiere. He slowly, deftly, flicked his thumbs over them, moving up and down, back and forth, making her moan and twist with need.

His hands on her breasts, his mouth never leaving hers, Steve slowly began to inch away from the door and into the room. Both were so absorbed in each other that Burton the cat crept unnoticed to stare curiously out the slightly opened door into the intriguing hall beyond. Carefully winding his way around their legs, he let out a triumphant meow as he successfully navigated his escape to freedom.

The sound's effect on Michelle was instantaneous. She pulled out of Steve's arms and flung the door open wide in time to see Burton racing down the hall. "Oh no! Burton, come back!" Her cry of distress echoed in the corridor as she went chasing after the cat.

Steve stared blindly ahead, feeling dazed and disoriented. One moment he had been holding her, kissing her, and suddenly he was left standing there alone, remembering the sweet hot taste of her mouth, the rounded softness of her breasts in his hands. His blood pulsed heavily. Every heartbeat made him throb with a desire and need that was painfully slow to subside.

It took several moments for him to shake off the impact of that potent languorous fog. Finally, heaving a sigh, he followed Michelle to the far end of the hall, catching up with her in the open stairwell.

"I don't know which way he went!" she cried, standing on the landing, looking first up and then down. "He won't come when I call him. He's so wound up. This is the first time he's ever been out of the apartment alone."

Steve stared at her. He was astonished to see that she was genuinely distraught. Her china blue eyes were swimming with unshed tears and she was visibly trembling. "Hey, he'll come back when he's ready," he soothed. "You know how cats are—they come and go as they please."

"No." Michelle shook her head, her voice choked. "Burton doesn't know his way around. I have to find him before he gets out of the building or he'll be hopelessly lost." She started to run up the stairs, then paused. "Will you help me find him, Steve?"

She was so agitated her voice was quavering. Steve was puzzled. Nothing in his experience warranted becoming upset because a cat had slipped out an open door. The Saraceni family had been letting their many cats in and out for years without a single bout of hysteria.

"Please!" cried Michelle. "I'll look on the third and fourth floors, if you'll take the first floor and the basement. And if the door to the building is open—"

"I'll close it," Steve finished for her. "Michelle, stop worrying. We'll find him." But she was already gone, presumably racing along the third-floor corridor in search of the runaway feline. Steve made his way to the first floor, shaking his head. Michelle was as high strung as her cat!

Although he felt no urgency, he checked the first floor of the building, and finding no sign of the cat, proceeded to the vestibule where he saw the front door swing closed. Obviously someone had just left the building.

Steve frowned. Had the cat taken advantage to zoom outside? He pushed the door open and called tentatively, "Here kitty, kitty," in what he hoped was a feline-enticing voice. He decided he sounded exceedingly foolish and didn't blame Burton for not responding. What self-respecting cat would?

"I checked the top floors and there was no sign of him." Michelle appeared by his side, her face pale, her voice frantic with worry. "Did he get out? He's never been outside before—only in his cat carrier when I take him to and from the car. He doesn't know about traffic or—"

"Michelle, calm down. He probably isn't outside and even if he is—"

"I've had him for almost three years." Michelle was crying now, tears streaming down her cheeks faster than she could wipe them away. "I got him when he was just six weeks old. I had to economize to afford him but I wanted him so much. I love cats and Burton is . . . he—he's special. If something happens to him, I—"

"Nothing is going to happen to him," Steve said firmly. But her anxiety was beginning to affect him. He was starting to feel slightly worried about the cat's whereabouts himself although he didn't dare let on. "Michelle, I'm going to search the basement and while I'm doing that, you go up to your apartment and put the cat's box outside your front door. Since he doesn't have any familiar scents around the building to guide him home, we'll provide him with one—his box."

Michelle nodded her head quickly, all the while trying to brush her tears away with her shaking hands. "Oh, yes, that's a good idea. Thank you. I'll do it right away."

Steve watched her race back up the stairs, two steps at a time. He had a feeling she was so desperate she would've said the same thing if he'd told her to drag a raw fish tied to a rope through the building.

The basement was dark and chilly, a long dark tunnel of locked doors. There was a light shining halfway down the hall and Steve briskly headed for it. He pushed open the partially closed door to find the laundry room. Inside were four washers and four dryers, a folding chair and a rickety car table. But no cat. Steve sighed, frustrated.

Michelle joined him. "I put the cat box out. Is Burton down here?"

Steve heard the note of hope in her voice. He hated to have to dash it. "No, he's not." Seeing the disappointment darken her vivid blue eyes hurt. "But I'm positive we'll have him soon, Michelle. The little devil is bound to be getting bored with his adventure by now."

His attempt to cheer her fell flat. "What if he *can't* come home?" Michelle whispered. "What if he's gone and I'll never see him again?"

"Michelle, that's not going to happen," Steve said sternly. "You have to stop thinking negatively and focus on—"

"It's happened before," she broke in tearfully, "to my other cat, my first cat, Fluffy. He was an albino cat, all white with pink eyes, and I had him for fourteen years. One morning—a few days after my high school graduation—I let him out, just like I always did. It was his daily routine, he'd spend about fifteen minutes outside and then want to come back inside. But when I went to the door to let him in, he wasn't there."

She gulped back a sob. "He wasn't anywhere. I looked all over for him. Every kid on the block helped me search the entire neighborhood all day long, but we never found him. He'd just vanished."

"Old cats do that when they're about to die," Steve said quietly. "They'll leave home and find a place to hide and—"

"That's what the vet told me. But it didn't help. It hurt so much to lose Fluffy that way. To have him just disappear and never see him again. I wondered if he was lost or scared or in pain—" Her voice broke.

"Michelle, come here, honey." Steve took her into his arms. He did not like sad stories and assiduously avoided them. How could one have a good time if one was encumbered by sadness? But at that moment he couldn't have walked away from Michelle any more than he could have abandoned one of his sisters when they were heartbroken or weeping. Except the feelings he had for Michelle as he held her close to him were decidedly not sisterly. His body was already beginning to react to her nearness.

Uh-oh! Every self-preservatory bachelor instinct he possessed went on red alert. It was definitely time to detach himself, to make a joke and break away. But he didn't.

"When I got Burton, I promised myself that I'd always keep him inside where he would be safe and I'd always know where he was," Michelle said softly, sadly, leaning into Steve, savoring the warmth and comfort he offered. "My heart broke every time I thought of Fluffy going off to die alone outside. He was such a good and faithful friend for fourteen years. Fluff went everywhere with me, when I visited my dad, no matter where he was stationed. As long as I had my cat, I felt I belonged to someone and that there was someone who really needed me around to—"

"Michelle, don't," Steve interrupted huskily. He was feeling her pain and it was unbearable.

He sought immediately to remedy it, with action. "We're going to find Burton," he said decisively, taking Michelle by the hand and half dragging her after him as he strode through the basement. "I'll comb the outside while you go door to door to every apartment in the building. There's a chance someone saw him, figured he was lost and took him in. But let's check your place first."

"He won't be there, I know it," Michelle murmured, squeezing back another round of tears.

"Come on now, it's time to start thinking positively." Steve pulled her to his side and wrapped his arm around her shoulders. "We're going to find your cat and we're going to find him very soon."

His confidence was bolstering, Michelle realized with some surprise. Maybe all wasn't lost, maybe there was some hope, after all.

They rounded the stairwell and entered the second floor. "Well, well, look who's home." Steve cupped Michelle's nape with his hand and turned her head toward the end of the hall. A Siamese cat was sitting in the box outside the door to her apartment.

"Burton!" Michelle took off at breakneck speed, rushing down the hall to scoop up the cat in her arms. "He's home!" she exclaimed, her face alight with joy. Burton meowed and began to purr loudly as she cuddled him close.

"I told you he'd soon tire of his great adventure and decide that there's no place like home," said Steve. His seeming nonchalance belied the genuine pleasure sweeping through him.

"Oh, Steve, thanks to you, Burton was able to find his way back!" Michelle exclaimed breathlessly. She gazed up at Steve with glowing eyes, her face radiant. "Your idea to put his cat box out by the door was—well, it was brilliant!"

"Like my driving, hmm?" He smiled, remembering she'd used the same superlative the night of the blizzard.

"Thank you so much for all your help, Steve!"

"Glad I could help." He particularly liked the way she was looking at him, her blue eyes shining with admiration and warmth, as if he were her hero.

Michelle carried the cat inside the apartment and Steve followed, gallantly bringing the cat box. He was careful to close the door tightly behind him. "We don't want another breakout," he said dryly. "Burton's used up his one allotted escape."

Burton wriggled in Michelle's arms, meowing a demand to be put down. Once on the ground, he circled the room in an excited dash, then ran toward the bedroom.

Steve chuckled. "Guess he's glad to be back."

Impulsively, Michelle gave him a quick hug. "Steve, I just can't thank you enough!"

He caught her arms as she was drawing away. "I know a way you could thank me."

Michelle immediately stiffened. "If you're going to suggest that I go to bed with you as a way to—"

"I wasn't," Steve interjected smoothly. "But I find it interesting that *you* suggested it."

"I most certainly did not!" She tried to pull away, but he used his superior strength to draw her closer.

"Don't get all riled up." Steve laughed huskily. "What I was about to suggest was going to New York with me this weekend. I have tickets for Friday's Rangers game and a friend has offered me two tickets for Saturday night to that new musical from London that's recently opened on Broadway. Will you come with me?"

Michelle met his eyes. "Yes."

"You will?" Steve was caught off guard. He'd been so sure she would refuse, he had been mentally preparing a list of reasons why she should accept his invitation. "Because you feel you owe me for the cat?" he asked uncertainly.

Michelle smiled. "Not really. I love New York. I can do some shopping there on Saturday afternoon and I also happen to like hockey games and musicals. It sounds like a great weekend. I'll be staying with my sister, of course."

He stared at her mutely.

"My stepsister Ashlinn lives in New York City. She's an editor for a travel magazine," Michelle explained. "I'm welcome to stay with her any time I want. I'll call and tell her to expect me this weekend."

"I see." She had neatly outmaneuvered him, Steve conceded.

"Does your invitation for the game and the show still stand?" she asked sweetly. "Or was it contingent upon sharing a room with you?"

"Of course my invitation still stands. You seem absolutely obsessed with the idea that *I'm* obsessed with getting you into bed." Nice save, Steve congratulated himself. He observed the flush pinking Michelle's cheeks with satisfaction. "I'll call you tomorrow night with more details, but we should try to leave Harrisburg by two o'clock Friday afternoon to make the game. Will you be able to get away then?"

Leaving the office a few hours early was unheard of for her, though other staffers did so, citing appointments, vacation plans and assorted other reasons. "Yes," she said confidently.

And she did. Brendan O'Neal kidded her about having a hot date. Claire expressed an interest but didn't press it when Michelle volunteered no information, and Leigh wasn't there because she'd left at noon for a weekend trip.

Steve picked up Michelle at two o'clock and stowed her bag and Burton, secure in his cat carrier and other cat gear in the car.

"I always take—" she began to explain.

"I know, I know. Wither thou goest, so goest your cat," Steve paraphrased. He wondered how they were going to get the cat into the hotel. Not for a moment did he believe that Michelle would be spending the weekend at her stepsister's place. Perhaps if he offered the bellhop a *very* generous tip, they could smuggle the cat into their room.

Traffic was light on the turnpike. "I'm glad we got an early start," Steve remarked. "At this rate, we should avoid the rush hour snarl around Philadelphia. Did you have any problem leaving the office early?"

Michelle shook her head. "I had a light schedule today. The committee for hazardous waste elimination met in the morning and then—"

"Any decisions on the locations of the sites?"

"Not exactly. But they did decide where the sites wouldn't be—in gamelands or forest preserves."

"And I'm relatively certain that there will be no hazardous waste elimination center in Ed Dineen's district," Steve drawled.

"Well, no."

"But I'd lay odds that a site in Joe McClusky's district is definitely being considered."

Michelle glanced at him in surprise. "There does happen to be an area in that district that would comply with all regulations," she said slowly.

"And what better way to stick it to your rival than to dump hazardous wastes in his district, hmm?" Steve shrugged. "I'm aware of the rivalry between Dineen and McClusky, Michelle."

"You're very cynical," Michelle said disapprovingly. "McClusky's district isn't the only site being seriously considered."

Steve merely shrugged again, a silent gesture of his disbelief.

"No, really," cried Michelle. She wanted to make him understand that Ed Dineen was no petty politician, striking his opponents with vengeful paybacks. To that end, she named several other sites being seriously considered as hazardous waste sites, all of them in politically neutral areas.

Smiling, Steve changed the subject before she had a chance to realize that she'd been indiscreet.

They spent the rest of the trip listening to tapes and talking desultorily about any number of subjects, and in what seemed a remarkably short time, they were on the outskirts of New York City.

Six

Michelle's stepsister Ashlinn lived in New York's upper west side in an old, somewhat seedy apartment building twelve stories high. Her apartment was on the eleventh floor and had four locks on the door.

"At least the elevator in this building works," Steve remarked as he and Michelle walked hand in hand along the dilapidated corridor toward Ashlinn's apartment. "I'd hate to have to trek up eleven flights of stairs."

His eyes flicked from the peeling paint on the walls to the almost threadbare carpet on the floor. "Are you sure you want to stay in this dump tonight? My room at the Plaza has a view of Central Park, a Jacuzzi and a bottle of champagne cooling on ice. Not to mention room service for midnight snacks and breakfast in bed."

Michelle stopped in front of Ashlinn's door. "Steve, I thought that you had—"

"—Given up trying to talk you into staying with me?" he interrupted ingenuously. "Now where would you get a ridiculous idea like that?'' He reached for her, taking her slowly, smoothly, in his arms. ''There are other things available tonight if you come with me, things you won't find here.''

Michelle looked up into his eyes, which were hot and searching, a sharp contrast to his light, casual tone of voice. ''Like what?'' she asked, her voice faintly husky.

Steve slipped his hands beneath her jacket and loose-fitting sweater. ''This,'' he murmured softly. He nuzzled her neck, tasting, caressing the sensitive skin there while his busy hands skimmed upward to unfasten the clasp of her bra with an expertise born of much practice.

''And this,'' he said raspily, covering her bare breasts with his hands. His lips brushed her mouth lightly, teasingly. ''There's a big, soft bed in that room.'' His thumbs lingered over her tight, tingling nipples. He nipped at her mouth gently. ''And I'll be in that bed, Michelle. I want you there with me.''

Michelle heard a quiet moan echo in the hall and realized that it had come from her. A heated knot in her stomach uncoiled, and warmth and moisture welled between her legs. And it was her arms that locked around his neck, her mouth hungrily seeking the depth and pressure of his, her tongue sliding between his lips.

Steve took over, kissing her with devastating thoroughness, using his practiced technique to arouse her. But there was nothing practiced about Michelle's wholehearted emotional response. She clung to him, kissing him with a breathless passion that sent him spinning out of his usual calculating, measured control.

Their kiss deepened and he was lost in the taste of her, drowning in the heady pleasure they shared. Heedless of their surroundings, he slid his hands to her bottom, squeezing and stroking her supple curves as he lifted her against his hard masculine heat.

It was the irritatingly loud, clanking sounds of the ancient elevator down the hall that finally intruded and broke the hot sensual spell enveloping them. Steve raised his head and gazed down at Michelle. She looked aroused and bemused, her blue eyes smoky and glazed with passion, her breasts rising and falling heavily with each breath she took. He couldn't resist tracing the outline of her lips, which were moist and red and slightly swollen from their kisses. Steve couldn't hold back his deep groan of arousal, of hunger and need.

"Michelle," he said hoarsely. "Baby, I—"

"I have to go in," she said quickly, pressing the doorbell, which sounded a melodious chime within. "Ashlinn is waiting for me."

He knew. He'd heard the discussion before he and Michelle left for the hockey game. Ashlinn didn't have extra keys for all four locks on her door, therefore she would have to wait up to let Michelle in. Steve hadn't challenged the arrangement at the time. He'd been absolutely certain that Michelle would be returning to the hotel with him.

She had been equally certain that she wouldn't.

The door was flung open and Michelle quickly moved away from him to say hello to her stepsister.

Steve had great difficulty summoning his customary charming grin of greeting. It didn't matter that the dark-haired, dark-eyed, sultry Ashlinn was stunningly sexy. His mind and his senses were too full of Michelle to notice any other woman. Ashlinn was a blur, an obstacle, and he wished she would disappear. He wanted to be alone with Michelle.

"Michelle, your cat drove me crazy all evening," Ashlinn announced. "He lounged on the manuscripts I was trying to read and attacked my pencil every time I tried to write. It would've been easier to work with a herd of elephants in the room than that one small cat."

"I'd better go," Steve interjected impatiently. His body felt as if it might explode—or implode. Whatever, he needed a cold shower, and soon. "I'll call you tomorrow, Michelle."

Michelle nodded her head, carefully not meeting his eyes.

"Do you have the telephone number here?" Ashlinn asked officiously.

Steve frowned irritably. Did the woman think he was a complete idiot? "Yes, Michelle gave it to me," he replied in the taut, long-suffering tone he used when one of his sisters asked him a particularly stupid question.

"Michelle and I plan to go shopping tomorrow, so call before ten or after four," Ashlinn ordered.

"I thought we were spending the day together, Michelle," Steve said, scowling. He'd counted on it. And after a full day of being treated to his charming company and irresistible sex appeal, she would be eager to crawl into bed with him.

"You're welcome to come shopping with Ashlinn and me," Michelle quickly assured him.

"Shopping?" Steve was aghast. "I hate shopping." Years of being dragged as a child from store to store by his mother and grandmother, of being forced to take his younger sisters to the mall after he'd received his coveted driver's license had taken its toll on him. Shopping—particularly shopping with women—was something to be avoided at all costs.

"You two go shopping, I'll find something else to do," he said, heaving a martyred sigh. "Good night."

"Your friend Steve didn't seem very happy," Ashlinn remarked with a laugh as she and Michelle went inside. "Was it the prospect of our shopping trip or did his team lose tonight?"

"It was the shopping because the Rangers won." Michelle sank down into a wide, comfortable armchair. Her face was flushed and her whole body was humming with unsated sexual tension. "The game was terrific. We really had a good time." She stared into space, her blue eyes thoughtful. "Even though Steve and I seem to fight a lot we do have a lot of fun together."

"It's my guess that smooth, sexy Steve didn't think he would have to bring you back here tonight," Ashlinn said gleefully. "He thought he could sweet talk you into going to his hotel room with him. I'm sure it came as a profound shock to find himself spending the night alone."

Michelle sighed. "I thought I'd made it very clear to him that I was staying here. After all, we'd already brought my suitcase and the cat here. I don't know why he would think otherwise."

"Hope springs eternal," Ashlinn said dryly. "Especially for a great-looking guy like him." She laughed. "Good for you, Michelle. In the battle of the sexes, you just won one for our side."

"I'm not a warrior or a crusader, Ashlinn. I just—"

"Did you have a fight when you insisted on coming back here to spend the night?" Ashlinn pressed.

Michelle shook her head no.

"Naturally, he's too smooth to fight. But I'm sure he let you know what you'll be missing." Ashlinn's dark eyes flashed. "Michelle, how deeply involved are you with him? Have you slept with him yet?"

Michelle shifted uncomfortably. She and Ashlinn were friends, but they'd never been confidantes. In the twenty-one years that they'd been stepsisters, they had never discussed sex or anything else that was remotely personal. It was disconcerting and rather embarrassing to do so now. "No, I haven't," she murmured.

"I'm afraid it's just a matter of time until you do," Ashlinn said frankly. "I saw the way he looks at you. He intends to have you. A smooth operator like him is used to getting whatever he wants from a woman. He's the type that firmly believes he has a license to love."

"I happen to have a say in the matter, too, you know," Michelle reminded her.

"Of course you do. And you're very strong-willed, you always have been. But there are some forces that can bend the strongest will, Michelle. Sex is one of them."

Michelle cleared her throat. "Thank you, I'll, er, keep it in mind," she said politely.

"You're probably thinking that I sound like one of those self-help books that proliferate the bestseller list."

Michelle smiled. "Maybe just a little."

"Actually, I am quoting from a self-help book. One that hasn't reached the bestseller lists yet, but hopefully will, as soon as it's finished. I'm writing that book, Michelle, but you must promise not to say a word to anyone yet."

"You're writing a book! Ashlinn, how exciting!" Michelle exclaimed. "But what about your job with the magazine?"

"Oh, I have no intention of quitting," Ashlinn said wryly. "I know enough about publishing to know that even bestselling authors ought to keep their day jobs unless they're one of a few mega stars. I'm doing this book in my spare time. I need a creative outlet and I had this inspiration for a book that I know will be a success. There's a crying need for it."

"Tell me about it," Michelle said eagerly.

Ashlinn flopped onto the sofa, her eyes shining with enthusiasm. "The title of my book is *Hooked!* The entire concept is the title. I'm compiling a collection of stories about women who've become sexually hooked on men, even if they're liars or narcissistic snakes or coldhearted users or any combination of those. The last quarter of the book will deal with the women's painful withdrawal from these men and their struggle for recovery."

"I don't want to put a damper on your plans, Ashlinn, but hasn't this book been written before, under different titles? At least ten times?"

Ashlinn frowned. "Well, there's always room for one more, especially with a high-concept theme like mine. The stories in my book are gripping—true experiences of women who are involved with men that are totally wrong for them in every way except sexually. Sex is the lure and the hook that keeps the woman helplessly trapped in the relationship. My premise is that when the sex is good between them, a woman can become so vulnerable and dependent on that man that nothing can set her free."

"But that can't really happen." Michelle gulped. "Can it?"

"It most certainly can. Sexual pleasure is such a powerful reward and reinforcer that a woman finds the man who gives it to her irresistible. And neither willpower nor common sense can set her free."

"Have you actually talked to any of these women? Do those relationships really exist or are you making it all up to sell your book?"

"I'm not making it up!" Ashlinn sounded aggrieved. "And yes, I've talked to a number of women who have been *Hooked!* I can personally vouchsafe for their stories."

Michelle's eyes widened. "Has it ever happened to you? Have you ever been involved in a relationship like that?"

"Of course not! What kind of a fool do you take me for? I think with my head, not with my hormones. I thought you did, too, but now I'm not so sure. Steve Saraceni is a sexual atomic bomb, Michelle. One blast and the fallout poisons your life forever."

Michelle winced. "That's a truly terrible analogy, Ashlinn. I hope you aren't going to use it in your book."

"It's from my book, Chapter One, and I think it's extremely apropos. I don't want to scare you, Michelle, but I do want to warn you to proceed with caution with your latest flame."

"He's not my latest flame." Michelle picked up Burton, who had begun to gnaw on a dried flower arrangement.

"But I appreciate your concern. I certainly don't want to end up hooked." She had to fight a smile. She'd forgotten how amusingly dogmatic and emphatic her stepsister could be when fighting her own self-styled crusade.

But as she lay awake that night on Ashlinn's torturously uncomfortable sofa bed, Michelle's amusement faded, to be replaced by chilling anxiety. She could make denials to Ashlinn, but she'd never been good at lying to herself. The truth was that she was in danger of falling in love with Steve.

She'd tried hard not to, but the longer she knew him, the more she liked him. He was easy and fun to talk to; he was dynamic and smart; he made her laugh. And she was so sexually attracted to him, she couldn't even think of him without becoming aroused and breathless.

His kisses evoked such powerful exciting passions within her, feelings that could only intensify if she were to give herself to him. Which was what making love with him would mean—giving herself to him, her heart and her soul along with her body. It couldn't be any other way for her and she knew it.

Add to that Ashlinn's foreboding theory of sexual pleasure as a lure and a hook, and her future appeared ominous indeed. Hooked! Deeply in love, needing and wanting a man who was so allergic to permanence and commitment that he couldn't even restrict his social life to one city. Vulnerable and dependent on Steve Saraceni, a man who didn't want love, just a good time.

Michelle shuddered. And made herself a promise. She was not going to become a true-life contributor to Ashlinn's book, sharing her gripping tale of hooked-on-heartbreak with anyone who plunked down the cover price.

"We had a great time this weekend, didn't we?" Steve settled himself down on the U-shaped sofa in Michelle's apartment, in no apparent hurry to leave. It was Sunday evening and they'd just returned to Harrisburg from New York.

Burton, delighted to be freed from his hours traveling in the cat carrier, raced manically around the apartment.

Michelle glanced at her watch. Nine o'clock. She usually took a shower and washed her hair at this time in order to get to bed early for a good night's sleep to begin the hectic week ahead. She watched as Steve picked up the Sunday paper and began to read.

Michelle felt a civil war break out inside her. She wanted him to leave as much as she wanted him to stay. She felt obliged to be polite but longed to evict him from the premises. And overriding everything else was an aching, yearning need to be in his arms again. Sensual memories of his kisses made her throb and burn for more. She stood on the threshold of the room, paralyzed with frustration and indecision.

"Uh-oh, look at this." Steve held up the paper for her to see. "There was a fire yesterday at the county animal shelter. Most of the animals were saved but now there's no place for them to go until the shelter is rebuilt."

The story was an instant lure. Michelle swiftly joined him on the sofa and together they looked at the page of photos of the displaced cats and dogs, kittens and puppies.

"'Officials are desperately urging people to adopt a pet at this time,'" Michelle read. "Hmm, I wonder how Burton would react to a kitten?"

"He might be a little testy at first, but the kitten would win him over," predicted Steve. "He'd love the company. Cats are basically quite sociable with other cats. I bet Burton gets lonely here with you gone all day at the office."

"I know he does. And I'd love to have a kitten..."

"Tomorrow, let's go to that warehouse where the animals are being temporarily kept. The place is open till eight. You can pick a kitten out."

"You want to go with me?" she asked incredulously. "Why?"

Steve shrugged. "Why not?"

She had no answer to that. He reached over and took her hand in his. "It was *interesting*—for lack of a better word— meeting your stepsister this weekend." He lifted her fingers to his mouth and meticulously kissed each tip, then skimmed the shaft of each finger with his lips. "She's a beautiful woman and seems quite fond of you—even though she hates me."

His sensual caresses made Michelle shiver with excitement. "Ashlinn doesn't hate you," she said huskily.

"She thinks I'm a cold, insincere smooth operator who'll use you and then break your heart. She told me so," he added as Michelle gave a small gasp of surprise, "when I came to pick you up this morning for brunch."

"Oh-ohh!" Michelle groaned. "Ashlinn's never been one to keep her thoughts to herself."

"I assume she shared her opinion of me with you, as well. It explains a lot."

"It does?" She looked at him. "Why? How?"

"You're so elusive. You let me so close, then bam, the walls go up and I'm on the outside looking in. Like last night, after the show. We had a wonderful time, we didn't want the evening to end, and it would've been perfectly natural for us to spend the night together. I know how much you want me but you won't let yourself go and—"

"I could say the same thing about you," Michelle interrupted. "Word for word, and it would apply."

"Don't be ridiculous. I'll go to bed with you the moment you say the word. Right now, if you want." He took her hand and laid it on his abdomen, just above his taut, straining masculinity. "I'm ready, willing and able, honey."

Michelle's heart jumped and she pulled her hand away. She could still feel the hard warmth of his body and a tingling heat streaked through her in response. Silently acknowledging the danger and the lure of being close to him, she rose to her feet, putting a much needed distance between them.

"You're talking about me and sex, I'm talking about you and commitment," she explained wearily. It was so hard to keep fighting what she was coming to want most. "You're right, I do want you but I won't let myself jump into bed with you just for the sport of it. And you want me, but you're just as reluctant to—to become seriously involved with me."

Steve stood up, too. "The age-old impasse." His eyes met and held hers. "If you don't give me what I need, there are other women who will. Is that what you want, Michelle? For me to go to someone else?"

"That creaky, ancient line isn't worthy of you, Steve." Michelle folded her arms in front of her chest and gazed at him impassively. "It was around when the Old Testament was being written. Please don't tell me that you've actually had success with it. Surely no woman today could be naive enough to—"

"Oh, you'd be surprised," Steve cut in. His face was slightly flushed. "But you do have a point—it is a tired old line." He grinned. "And I respect you for not buying it."

Michelle shook her head. "You really are incorrigible, you know."

"And you're equally intractable, sweetheart," he said pleasantly. He walked to the door. "Come here and kiss me goodbye, Michelle. Then I'll be on my way." His dark eyes were gleaming, his expression and his tone challenging.

And Michelle couldn't resist. She went to him, stood on tiptoe and swiftly pecked his cheek.

Steve's arms instantly encircled her, pressing her firmly against him and keeping her there. "I said kiss me goodbye and I'll be on my way," he repeated silkily. "But not before or until."

Her heart was pounding very fast. "I did." She looked up at him from beneath her lashes, her gaze seductive, her voice softly provocative. Her behavior astonished her. She'd never indulged in flirtatious games. How and why did they seem to come so naturally to her now?

A slow smile curved the corners of Steve's mouth. "Try again, baby."

Impulsively, wildly, in a move that was totally uncharacteristic for her inhibited, conservative self, Michelle's open mouth sought his. Steve's response was instantaneous.

He gripped her fiercely. Her mouth was warm and sweet and eager, and his body ignited like a blowtorch. Wanting her with an ever-mounting passion and urgency, he angled her closer to him, fitting the hard male planes of his body to the supple feminine softness of hers. His tongue penetrated her mouth deeply, moving in and out in excruciating sexual simulation.

Their kisses, tempestuous and passionate, from the start grew even longer, deeper and hungrier. When it was impossible to remain standing for another moment, they drew breathlessly apart. Steve had an overwhelming urge to sweep her up in his arms and carry her to bed. It was a ridiculous, quixotic and romantic gesture he'd never made before, yet it seemed natural with her, for her. He'd carried her in the snow and he'd carried her the night of the blizzard when she'd been too afraid to go into the bedroom herself.

Of course, he would carry her to bed the first time they made love.

"This—is getting dangerous." Michelle's shaky voice drew him from his languid, sensual reverie.

"What do you mean?" His fingers toyed lazily with the top button of her blouse.

"We're at cross purposes. At an impasse. You said so yourself." He wanted sex for fun and she wanted sex with love. "I don't see a solution." She pushed his hand away and moved out of his reach.

Steve sighed. "You're letting yourself be influenced by your stepsister. Don't let her opinion of me govern your—"

"I'm perfectly capable of making my own decisions, without being unduly influenced by anyone, let alone Ashlinn."

"Okay. Okay." Steve held up both hands in a gesture of surrender. "So it's your own idea to turn on and off quicker than a light switch. A very effective torture, I might add. I've taken so many cold showers since I met you that I could qualify for membership in the Polar Bear Club."

"Why suffer the cold showers when there are all those women who will give you what you need?"

He should be angry, he should be snapping right back at her. Steve pondered the fact that he wasn't. Michelle was spoiling for a quarrel; she was deliberately baiting him. Why wasn't he giving her exactly what she was asking for? Maybe because he knew that what she really wanted wasn't to send him away in anger? She wanted what he wanted—to make love. She just hadn't realized it yet. But she would, and very soon, he would see to that.

"No fair throwing my creaky old lines back in my face," he replied, grinning. Though she was scowling and sniping at him, he felt an inexplicable tenderness toward her that should have alarmed him. For some equally inexplicable reason, it didn't.

"I'll pick you up shortly before seven tomorrow night and we'll go get a kitten. We can pick up some take-out Chinese for dinner on the way back."

He gave her a swift, hard kiss and was gone, leaving a confused, bemused Michelle staring at the closed door for a long time afterward.

"What are you going to name her?" Steve asked, glancing at the three pound, seven-week-old calico kitten that Michelle held in her lap. Burton, crouched at the other end of the sofa, was staring at the tiny intruder, his back arched, his tail six times the normal size.

"I don't know." Michelle watched the kitten climb purposefully across her lap to stand on the sofa cushion beside her. "Courtney named Burton. Her first assignment for National Public Broadcasting was a piece on Sir Richard Burton, the British explorer and Orientalist, not the actor. She thought it a very fitting name for an adventuresome, Oriental cat, and I had to agree."

The calico kitten trotted purposefully toward the older cat. When Burton hissed threateningly, she opened her tiny pink mouth, emitted a barely audible sound, and hastily retreated to Michelle's lap.

Steve laughed. "She can't even work up a full-fledged meow, just a little squeak."

"Squeaky. That's her name," Michelle decided. She watched the kitten make another overture to Burton, only to be rebuffed again. "Do you really think Burton will adjust to her?" she asked worriedly.

"I guarantee it. Keep the kitten closed in your bedroom while you're at work, though. The two of them can get acquainted through the crack under the door. When we're home, they can both have the run of the place. I predict that within a week, these two will be on the way to becoming best friends."

When *we're* home, he'd said. Michelle gazed at him curiously. He didn't even realize the slip. She wasn't about to point it out to him.

The cat and the kitten were the focal point of the evening. It wasn't until both had curled up—separately—to sleep that Steve glanced at his watch. "Ten o'clock. Want me to leave or are you up for a wrestling match on the couch that will undoubtedly lead to another cold shower for me?"

"Wouldn't you be surprised if I opted for the wrestling match?" She kept her voice as light as his.

"You'd like to, wouldn't you, Michelle? In fact, you want me to stay as much as I do. One of these days you'll admit it, to yourself and me."

"And then you can put another notch on the old bedpost and move on. You'd like that, wouldn't you, Steve?"

He laughed. "Baby, I'm living for that glorious day. Meanwhile, I'll be over tomorrow evening—if that's okay with you," he added as an afterthought.

"You will? Why?"

Good question, Steve commended silently. "I want to see the kitten," he said aloud. He decided it was true. "I get a kick out of seeing her and Burton. I like cats a lot, you know. I grew up with them and I miss not being around them."

"Why not get some cats of your own?" suggested Michelle, as one cat fancier to another. "You could get a couple kittens from the temporary shelter. There are so many there and—"

"It wouldn't be fair for me to have pets. Not with my schedule. I'm rarely home."

"And the thought of having a living, breathing presence at home eagerly waiting for you makes you nauseated," Michelle said coolly. For just a moment, she'd been on the verge of forgetting his commitment phobia. He wouldn't even commit to a houseplant, much less a cat. A woman didn't stand a chance with this man.

But when he appeared at her door the following evening with a pepperoni pizza, she invited him in. She was delighted to see him and couldn't hide it. Being with him was exhilarating. Simple things like watching the news on TV or playing with the cats took on a whole new, richer dimension when shared with Steve.

The days and weeks passed. February turned into March, March into April. Steve and Michelle fell into a pattern of sorts. They spent at least two evenings a week together, quiet evenings with dinner at an informal restaurant or at her apartment eating take-out or some simple dish she'd prepared. Sometimes they rented videos and watched them, sometimes they simply listened to music and talked. There didn't seem to be a topic they couldn't or didn't discuss, although the machinations of state politics was always a favorite. Burton and Squeaky, now best friends despite the disparity in their sizes, ages and sex, continued to provide entertainment.

Steve's schedule included a host of dinners, fund-raisers and meetings, which he usually attended alone. Michelle didn't mind. Those were working nights for him and she understood the demands of a lobbyist's continual quest for access and information.

Weekends were different. For several weeks, Steve continued his out-of-town weekend excursions and Michelle remained in Harrisburg. When he called and came over on Sunday nights, as he invariably did, she was careful not to ask anything about where he'd been, what he'd done and with whom. She didn't know if he was dating other women and he didn't volunteer the information, which was fine with her. She didn't want to know.

By the middle of March, he was spending Friday evenings with her; by the end of that month, they were going out on Saturday nights, too, to dinner alone or with friends, to the movies, to parties. On the Harrisburg scene, they were considered a couple, although Michelle was certain that Steve wasn't aware of it. She was convinced that he also didn't realize how much time they were spending together. It had come about so gradually, so naturally.

And the more time they spent together, the hotter and higher the sexual attraction between them flamed. Their kisses and caresses became more passionate, more intimate and meaningful. Steve made it clear that he wanted to make love with her and often pressured her, sometimes subtly, sometimes not, but he never tried to force her or threaten her when she refused. He accepted her decision without sulking or raging.

"You're fighting yourself right now, honey, not me," he said confidently, and Michelle knew he was probably right. She waited for him to grow bored with her, but he kept coming around. If he was biding his time, waiting for her inevitable surrender, Michelle knew he wouldn't have to wait much longer.

She was in love with him, and all those valid reasons she'd used to keep him out of her bed seemed less relevant and completely inapplicable when compared to how much she cared for him. And he cared for her, too, she was certain that he must, although he'd never actually said so. But she took comfort in the adage about "actions speaking louder than words."

If he didn't care, he wouldn't spend so much time with her.

If he didn't care, he wouldn't defer his sexual demands to her wishes.

If he didn't care, he wouldn't gaze at her with such warmth and admiration in his dark velvety eyes; he wouldn't laugh at her jokes no matter how lame; he wouldn't call her on those evenings they didn't spend together, just to tell her about his day and hear about hers.

But Steve did all those things and Michelle's love for him grew as her desire for him intensified. When—she knew now that it was *when* not *if*—they made love, it would be her decision based on her own free will rather than the successful result of one of Steve's smooth seductions. That was important to her. She wanted to be his partner, not his target. She wanted to be *the* one for him, not merely one of his fungible conquests.

Michelle allowed herself to dream that she was the one woman in the world for him, the special and lasting love of his life. And slowly and steadily, her dream became her belief. She really was his love and it was only a matter of time before he knew it, too.

Seven

April

"**M**ichelle, this is Steve."

She knew at once that something was wrong. Steve never identified himself over the phone, he always assumed that she'd recognize his voice. Of course, he was quite right, she always did. And after all those long, lazy hours on the telephone with him, she was attuned to every nuance in his voice. Today he sounded tense and uneasy.

"I, uh, I'm going to have to cancel for tonight."

Michelle swallowed, hard. "Oh?"

"Something's come up," Steve said tightly. "I won't be able to make it."

He paused and she waited for him to continue. He didn't. A shiver of apprehension rippled through her. *That was it?* Without any further explanation, he was canceling the small dinner party that she'd planned with his partners, Greg Arthur and Patrick Lassiter and their girlfriends, Stacey and Julia, to celebrate his thirty-fourth birthday?

Disappointment rolled over her. She'd already planned the menu, bought the food and cleaned her apartment. Patrick and Julia were bringing the birthday cake, Greg and Stacey the wine, and she was about to start cooking the dinner.

But she decided to give him the benefit of the doubt. "Steve, are you sick?" she asked concernedly.

"No." His voice was clipped. "I'm—" he cleared his throat, then added coolly " —sorry about this, Michelle."

He was standing her up for the birthday party she'd planned for him, without offering a single reason, and he had the nerve to merely say he was "sorry"? And he didn't even sound particularly sorry, at that.

"So am I," Michelle said. Her tone was as cool as his and completely belied the pure, unadulterated fury bubbling up inside her. "But we'll toast you and sing Happy Birthday to you in your absence."

There was a momentary shocked silence on Steve's end of the line. "You're going ahead with the dinner? Without me?"

"Of course. The arrangements have already been made. I see no reason to change plans at the last minute."

"No reason?" His voice rose. "It was a birthday dinner for me and I won't be there! Isn't that reason enough?"

"Oh, you'll be here in spirit. When we light the candles on the cake, we'll all be thinking of you."

"There will only be five at the table," Steve reminded her testily. "Two couples and you. Talk about feeling like a fifth wheel!"

"Hmm, I suppose I could always call Brendan O'Neal from the office, and invite him to come over. He's always broke, always hungry and always happy to accept a free meal. He would make six, an even number of wheels."

"You'd invite another man to take my place at my own birthday party?" Steve was incensed and made no attempt to conceal it.

"Brendan isn't *another man,*" Michelle said airily, mocking his dramatic intensity. "He's just a student and he happens to be a very good friend of mine who—"

"He's a law student, only a couple of years younger than you, not a schoolboy," Steve interrupted caustically. "Don't kid yourself, Michelle. O'Neal is a *man* and inviting him to your apartment is tantamount to a come-on. As for that good friends bit, hah! Maybe on your part, baby, but not on his. I've been in your office, I've seen the way he practically slavers and pants over you."

Michelle actually laughed. Her relationship with Brendan O'Neal had always been—and continued to be—purely platonic. But her laughter took on a hard edge as she snapped, "Brendan doesn't pant over me! It's the dim-witted women you date in four different cities who do the panting over you whenever you do them the honor of showing up for a night of—of meaningless sex."

"You're the only woman I've dated in months, dim-witted or otherwise," Steve snarled. "Furthermore, I haven't had *any* sex since I met you. Lord knows, I practically have to chase you around the room for a good-night kiss."

It was hardly an accurate description of the increasingly passionate, intense necking sessions that they indulged in at least twice a week, but Steve was too outraged to be either accurate or fair and Michelle was too dumbfounded by his impromptu admission to call him on it. *He hadn't slept with anyone since way back in January, when they'd met? He hadn't dated others during the early months of their relationship, when she had gloomily assumed he was still pursuing other women?*

A long silence hung between them. Steve was the first to break it. "Look, I have to go," he muttered, and hung up without saying goodbye.

Michelle carefully replaced the receiver in its cradle, restraining the impulse to slam it down with bone-jarring force. There was no use punishing the telephone, which was, after all, only an inanimate instrument communicating infuriating messages. That would be as irrational as the old custom of killing the bearer of bad tidings. But for the first time, Michelle truly understood the motivation behind it.

She was standing there, debating whether or not to call off the dinner or to invite Brendan to come to it, deciding whether to rage or to cry when the phone rang again. She answered it reflexively.

"Michelle, I'm not bowing out tonight on a capricious whim," Steve said, he voice calm and smooth and reasonable once more. "I had hoped you would realize that instead of staging a possessive tantrum."

"I didn't," Michelle fired back. "*You* did. You accused Brendan O'Neal of lusting after me. And if the reason you called back is to rehash or prolong the argument, I'd prefer to hang up now."

She could almost hear him clench his jaw as he clenched, "I called back because I decided I should tell you why I can't make it tonight."

"How big of you!"

"It would serve you right if I hung up right now without another word," Steve said grimly. But he didn't. He was well aware that failing to appear at a party being held in one's honor was unconscionably rude unless one had a faultlessly acceptable excuse, neurosurgery or death being two of the very few in that category.

"The truth is that my family arrived here unexpectedly," he continued, loosing a sigh. "They had some furniture to bring to my cousin Saran and decided to combine the trip with a birthday visit to me. They're all over at Saran's place right now, but they'll be back here for dinner. The entire family is here—my parents, my grandmother, Cassie and her kids, Jamie and Rand and the baby. They brought enough lasagna, ravioli, braciola, *saltine bocca, foccacia* and salad to feed both houses of congress."

"You should've told me in the first place," Michelle said quietly. "Of course you can't leave them. I—I'll call the others and explain."

"Michelle, the food you bought for the dinner to-night..." Steve took a deep breath. "I know it was expensive. I want to reimburse you for it."

"Don't be silly. I can freeze everything." Michelle did not presume to suggest the logical alternative—that she join his family at his place for the birthday dinner. She'd known him long enough and well enough to realize that Steve Saraceni kept his social life entirely separate from his family. An introduction to the Saraceni clan was not in the cards for her tonight. Dispiritedly, she wondered if it ever would be.

"Have a good time tonight, Steve," she said, mustering credible cheer. "Oh, and happy birthday."

"Thanks, babe." He was smooth and smiling again; she could hear it in his voice. Steve expected things to go easily for him and was rarely disappointed. "I'm really sorry about the dinner," he added. "If you'd like, I'll call Greg and Patrick myself and explain."

"Never mind, I'll do it."

But instead of calling his partners, Michelle called their girlfriends, Julia and Stacey, whom she'd gotten to know well since dating Steve.

"He didn't even invite you to have dinner with them?" Julia exclaimed after Michelle told her that the dinner was off and why. "That jerk!"

"I can't believe he didn't suggest that you join him and his family for the birthday dinner!" Stacey was equally irate on Michelle's behalf. "What a thoughtless creep!"

Michelle had to agree. She'd needed to vent some steam over Steve's cavalier dismissal and it was something of a soothing balm to hear her own thoughts verified. But following her bout of self-righteous anger, there came a deep and searing hurt. How could she delude herself into believ-

ing that he cared about her when he wouldn't even invite her
to his birthday dinner?

Well, thought Michelle, *I can sit around here and mope
like a pitiful creature who's been* Hooked! *or I can take my
life into my own hands.* She opted for the latter. It was
April, she'd recently read an article about the cherry blos-
soms being in gorgeous full bloom in the nation's capital
where her stepsister Courtney happened to live. She hadn't
seen Courtney for a while and, suddenly, it seemed an ideal
time to visit her.

Several phone calls later, Michelle's plans were in gear.
She arranged for a few vacation days from work and her
neighbor agreed to keep Squeaky whom Michelle deemed
too young to travel. Besides, springing a lively kitten, plus
Burton, on Courtney who was politely indifferent to cats at
best, didn't seem quite fair.

Within an hour of Steve's cancellation, the food for his
birthday dinner was in the freezer and Michelle and Burton
were on the interstate highway heading toward Washington.

"And how was your day, Burtie?" Michelle asked the cat
upon entering Courtney's apartment. Burton meowed a
greeting and followed her into the bedroom.

"I think that a full day of sightseeing is more exhausting
than a forty hour work week." She kicked off her shoes as
she spoke, then peeled off her pantyhose. It felt good to flex
her cramped, bare toes in the soft pile of the carpet.

"Before I fix myself a cup of tea and get you a kitty treat,
I want to show you the prints I bought for my bedroom."
Michelle removed the reproduction prints of the original
masterpieces from the paper bag marked National Gallery
of Art. She'd made her purchases in the gift shop after
viewing the paintings in the cavernous art museum, her sixth
and final tourist stop of the day. She'd ended with dinner in

a small restaurant near the White House, then caught the Metro back to Courtney's apartment.

Burton was unimpressed with the art. His attention was focused on a furry gray toy mouse that he hunted with the same tactical concentration as a big cat in the wilds. Both were so engrossed—Michelle with her prints and Burton with his mouse—that neither made any response the first time the doorbell rang.

When the ringing persisted, Burton froze and tilted his head, cocking his ears. Michelle looked equally quizzical. "Who could that be?" she wondered aloud. "Courtney couldn't be expecting anyone, she's out of town. And couriers don't make evening deliveries, do they?"

Tentatively, she went to the front door and reached to open the small metal door that covered the square metal-barred peephole. Michelle uttered a small gasp. Were her eyes playing tricks on her?

"Steve?" Her voice rose to an incredulous squeak.

Steve's eyes flew to the small opening in the door where he saw and heard Michelle through the crossed metal bars. "Of course it's me. Who were you expecting, the Easter Bunny?"

Michelle was operating on pure astonishment as she automatically opened the door. "But how—" she began.

He gave her no chance to finish. He pushed his way inside, pulled her roughly into his arms and bent his head to hers, capturing her mouth with one fell swoop. The door slammed behind them. For one startled moment, Michelle stood rigid and still in his arms as her spinning mind attempted to assimilate his presence.

Steve wasn't waiting for her to come to grips with his sudden appearance. His mouth was open and hard on hers, his kiss angry and punishing, a primitive display of possessive male dominance, and the effect on Michelle was oddly paradoxical. She wanted both to rebel and to submit.

And then her most primal feminine instincts took over, responding to the hard strength of his arms and the warm pressure of his body against hers. Her lips parted on a small sigh and the hot taste of his mouth filled her. Michelle thrust her fingers into the dark thickness of his hair and fervently kissed him back.

As soon as Steve felt the melting warmth of her response, the whole nature of the kiss changed. Anger gave way to pure passion and he kissed her with a hungry urgency that revealed a desperate desire.

His hands gathered her skirt and lifted it. His big, warm palm glided up her bare thigh. When he encountered the lacy edges of her panties, he shuddered with arousal, then cupped her bottom with both hands, kneading and caressing the firm, silk-covered softness.

Michelle's breath caught on a moan and her back arched. She moved against his hands as a river of sensual pleasure eddied through her. She wrapped her arms around his muscled shoulders and hugged him tighter to her, wanting to be as close as she could. Part of her wondered if she were dreaming a very erotic dream. His sudden appearance seemed like an awesome combination of fantasy and wish fulfillment.

But her swimming senses validated the reality of his presence. She could feel the heat of his body and smell the male muskiness of his skin. His body was hard and taut under her hands, and the sound of his deep, rasping breaths filled her ears.

His mouth left hers to gently suck the sensitive cord of her neck, and Michelle whimpered as the sensation evoked a corresponding tingling heat in her breasts and deep in her belly. Her nipples beaded and throbbed, a syrupy warmth pooled between her thighs.

"I can't believe you're really here," she whispered feverishly, clinging to him as if he might disappear if she let him go.

"I'm here." His voice was deep and low and husky, and the very sound of it excited her. "Don't tell me to leave, Michelle."

It was debatable as to whether his impassioned reply was an order or a plea. Michelle didn't care either way. Sending him away was unthinkable. When he lifted her slightly, to settle her harder and higher against him, graphically demonstrating her effect on him, she undulated her hips in response to the carnal pressure.

"I want you to stay," she said softly. Once she said the words, she knew there was no turning back. And she didn't want to. It was time. She was in love and she'd missed him, even though he'd hurt her with his cavalier treatment the night of his birthday.

But that was in the past, and her nature was too generous and giving to nurture a grudge. She gazed into his burning black gaze. Her heart was pounding and her body pulsated with an aching sexual tension that throbbed just as wildly in him.

Steve's chest rose with a swift, deep intake of breath and he picked her up in his arms. The apartment was small and he carried her to the bedroom, finding it easily.

A dark flash of fur brushed his legs as he laid her down on the bed, and he jerked upright, startled. "What the—"

"It's Burton playing with his mouse," Michelle explained. "I guess we intruded on his game and he left in a huff."

Steve managed a shaky laugh. "You and your crazy cats and your crazy trips and your crazy—"

"I get the point," Michelle interrupted huskily, reaching for him. "You think I'm crazy."

He came down beside her with a rough groan. "You make *me* crazy." His mouth covered hers with breathtaking impact.

The taste of him went straight to her head, and Michelle welcomed the bold penetration of his tongue, needing him in the most elemental way, craving union with him, body, heart and soul.

He unbuttoned her blouse and unclipped her bra with ardent, arousing hands. She lay trembling and vulnerable, her breasts bared to him, watching his dark eyes study her with blazing intensity. Her body was on fire, empty and aching, wanting something she had never known but instinctively hungered for.

Steve gazed at the flawless ivory smoothness of her full breasts, her taut raspberry nipples. His mind was rioting, his body rigid with a pleasure so fierce it bordered on pain. He'd waited longer for Michelle than he had ever had to wait for anything or anyone. He was used to things coming easily to him, to people doing what he wanted and when.

Waiting for Michelle's capitulation these past months had certainly not been easy. She was a challenge that he rarely faced. But the sight of her lying there, her blue eyes filled with passion and yearning, her pretty breasts rising and falling softly under his gaze, more than fulfilled the torturous anticipation of waiting.

"You're so beautiful," he said hoarsely. "So sexy. And I want you so much that I—I—" His mind went blank, hot licks of passion erasing his usual ready supply of stock lines.

Steve bent his head and took the tight rosy peak in his mouth, gently laving it with his tongue, then drawing it deeper, sucking and nibbling, until Michelle was squirming and arching and shuddering with pleasure.

"It feels so good," she heard herself murmur in a throaty, sexy voice that she hardly recognized as her own. Her eyes were tightly closed. It felt almost *too* good. The intensity of the tempestuous, voluptuous sensations sweeping through her made her feel dizzy and dazed and completely out of control.

It was wild, scary and exhilarating at the same time. She felt his fingers at her waist, manipulating the button and zipper of her skirt, then deftly divesting her of it. Her bikini panties were dark blue with white stars on them. Steve's lips curved into a lazy, sensual smile.

"Patriotic," he drawled.

Michelle blushed. "I—I'm partial to stars and stripes and anything red, white and blue," she felt obliged to explain. "Maybe because I come from a military family."

"I won't be able to look at Old Glory again without thinking of these." His eyes gleaming, he slid his hand over the fabric.

She felt chary and exposed and so very vulnerable. "Don't tease me, Steve."

Her shyness touched him. "I wasn't teasing you," he said softly, his lips feathering the creamy smooth flatness of her belly. "Well, maybe just a little." His tongue circled her navel. "Serves you right for pulling that disappearing act."

"Disappearing act?" she echoed drowsily. Her mind was spinning, and she was having difficulty keeping the threads of the conversation straight.

"I've been trying to track you down since Saturday night. It was as if you'd vanished." Steve frowned, remembering. "I was madder than hell."

"At me?"

He audaciously inserted the tip of his tongue into her navel's tiny hollow depth. Michelle gasped. When his hand moved between her legs, cupping her intimately, she uttered a soft cry.

"At myself," Steve admitted gruffly. He rubbed her, watching as she shivered helplessly under his fingers. "For being a jackass and for letting you get away."

"But you found me," she managed to whisper. Her breath caught and held as he slipped his big, warm hand inside her panties.

"I found you," he echoed huskily. His fingers combed through the luxuriant triangle of dark blond curls, gliding along the exquisite folds of feminine softness.

She blushed at the swollen wet heat he found there. Then he was kissing her again, as wildly and hungrily as before, and her embarrassment was dissolved in a storm of intoxicating passion. He slid her panties down the length of her body and opened her legs farther with his hand. Caressing her with light, gliding touches, exquisitely probing, he penetrated the hot secrets of her body.

Michelle cried his name and clutched his shoulders, unconsciously digging her nails into the muscled strength. What he was doing to her...how he was touching her...the way he made her feel . . . She'd never experienced anything so profoundly intimate. She felt delirious, as with fever, but she never wanted it to stop. She didn't want him to stop.

And he didn't. Slowly, carefully, as if he had all the time in the world, he concentrated on pleasuring her, with his lips and his hands, gauging her responses and tailoring his caresses to suit them. Repeating, intensifying, taking her higher and higher. She moaned, her whole body shuddering as each tender penetration and gliding withdrawal stretched the burgeoning tension within, until it burst into shimmering waves of heat, so pleasurable that emotional tears streamed down her cheeks.

Through her convulsive sensual daze, she could hear Steve's voice, exultant and male and proud. "Yes, baby. That's it. Just let go..."

Her whole body felt bathed by a glowing warmth and Michelle lay limp in Steve's arms, feeling too languorous to even open her eyes.

"I didn't dream you'd be so responsive." Steve brushed light, biting kisses over her cheeks, her forehead, her lips.

Michelle's eyelids fluttered open. She gazed at him with wide, wondrous blue eyes. And then a dark blush swept over her. She was in bed with him, naked, while he was still fully clothed. And her unbridled responses to the intimacies he had performed on her made her flinch with self-conscious embarrassment.

"You—didn't?" She didn't know what to do, what to say. Her inexperience was so blindingly obvious to herself, she was sure it must be apparent to Steve, as well. "Why not?"

Steve smiled. "It crossed my mind that you might find it difficult to give in and lose control. You've certainly demonstrated your ability to *keep* control and call a halt whenever—"

"Do we have to have a postmortem?" Michelle interrupted, flinching. Her blush deepened.

Steve stared in fascination as her white skin turned a warm pink. "I've never seen anyone blush from head to toe. You, my sweet, are an ever-surprising phenomenon."

Michelle winced. If this was bedroom banter, she knew she wasn't going to be good at it. Better complete silence than trading these shatteringly intimate observations. Even worse, she had none to trade. He'd done everything while she had simply lain there.

Steve saw the anxiety shadow her face and correctly interpreted the consternation flickering in her eyes. He cupped her cheek with his hand, gently stroking the soft skin with his fingertips. "What is it, sweetheart?"

"It's just—after that—" She paused, took a deep breath and tried again. "I don't know what to say to you," she admitted hesitantly.

"Say whatever you want. There is no script we have to follow, Michelle." He rolled on top of her, pinning her down on the mattress, adjusting his body to hers so she could feel the insistent heat of his arousal. "Although I could offer a few suggestions. How about, 'Oh Steve, you're a marvelous lover!'" he trilled in a ridiculous falsetto. His dark eyes glittered with an irresistible combination of humor and passion. "Or, 'Steve, you're my hunka hunk of burning love,' will do nicely, too."

Michelle laughed, her insecurity dissolving in a barrage of more powerful emotions and sensations. "I love you," she whispered. Those were the words she'd been looking for. And they were surprisingly easy to say.

Steve didn't react to her declaration; she hadn't expected him to. It might be the first time she'd made an impassioned claim of love, but she knew it wasn't Steve's first time to hear one. A man with his looks, charm and sex appeal, combined with his ability to use all three to his advantage would've been hearing ''I love yous'' from amorous females since elementary school.

Such thoughts were disquieting and disturbing, but she pushed them away. This was no time to get cerebral. She loved Steve, faults and all, in spite of his past.

Michelle wrapped her arms around Steve, holding him tightly. The starched cloth of his shirt rubbed her bare breasts. Her nipples were almost unbearably sensitive. His trouser-clad legs were entwined with her naked limbs and she was once again erotically, arousingly aware that she was nude and he was not. That sharp, secret throbbing that had been eased only a few moments before began to build again.

''Take off your clothes,'' she murmured, rather amazed at her own boldness. But this was no time for an attack of virginal nerves. She was a mature woman with the man she loved, the man she'd been waiting for her entire life. The man who would soon become her lover. She slipped her hands between their bodies and tried to undo the buttons on his shirt.

Steve rolled on his side and ably assisted her in divesting himself of his shirt. She was relieved when he continued to undress on his own, though she watched with wide, avid eyes. Her pulses were racing. She felt wired with excitement, her skin tingled and an aching warmth swelled and throbbed deep within her.

She drew a sharp breath at the sight of his nude body. He was splendid, powerful, male and strong, with corded arms, and a muscular chest covered with an intriguing dark, curly mat that tapered to a V at his navel and then arrowed downward. His stomach was flat, his thighs, long, lean and powerfully muscled. And it was visibly apparent that he wanted her very much.

Michelle wanted to touch him, to feel his strength and his hardness, to explore the contrasting textures of his smooth skin and wiry masculine pelt. She reached out her hand to him, welcoming, beckoning, her smile as timeless as Eve's.

Steve sat down on the edge of the bed and looked at her for a long moment. "I've never wanted a woman as much as I want you right now," he said. "Hell, I've never wanted *anything* as much as I want you."

He lay down beside her, propping himself up on one elbow so he could watch her as he skimmed his other hand along the shapely length of her body. He wanted her desperately, but the anticipatory torment was so delicious in itself that he held himself back.

For now, he limited himself to the pleasures of looking at her, of touching her where his eyes strayed. The plump fullness of her pretty pink and white breasts, the hollow of her waist and womanly curve of her hips. Her thighs were femininely rounded, her legs well shaped. He smoothed his hands along the outside of them, then slipped between them, gliding upward to the creamy softness of her inner thighs.

Michelle moved sinuously, sensuously under his hands, unable to lie still, wanting and aching and needing to give. It was no longer enough to lie submissively as he petted her; she needed to give him pleasure, to learn his body as he was learning hers.

She framed his face with her hands, then touched her mouth to his, again and again in a series of sweet, soft kisses. Using the tip of her tongue, she traced the outline of his lips, then slipped between them to tease his tongue into a caressive little duel.

"Michelle," he groaned her name. She rarely took the initiative physically, letting him make the first move, be it kisses or caresses. Now her passionate feminine aggression sent him reeling. It was an effort to speak at all with the powerful coil of desire tight and sharp within him, consuming him with need.

"I can't wait any longer." Hadn't he already waited a lifetime for her? It felt that way, as if his life hadn't really begun until she'd entered it. The thought was so profound and so unsettling that he quickly blocked it out, concentrating instead on the incredible, unbelievable storm of pleasure her soft hands were evoking within him. For she had found the pulsating male strength of him and was scrupulously exploring the size, shape and length with her fingertips.

"Here." Twisting, reaching, he grabbed his slacks that he'd dropped on the floor and retrieved a foil packet from the pocket. He thrust it into Michelle's hand. "Put this on."

Michelle stared at it bewilderedly. Then the light dawned and she nearly giggled. "For a moment or two, I wasn't sure what you meant. You see, I've never—helped a man put on a condom before."

Steve took the packet from her. "That's okay, honey. I'll do it. It's probably just as well. I think I'll explode if you touch me again."

Michelle watched, fascinated, as he sheathed himself with astonishing efficiency. It occurred to her that she hadn't given a thought to protection and she was grateful that Steve had. Vaguely, she recalled his frantic fears of learning that he might be "eligible for a tie and a card on Father's Day" through sexual carelessness. She certainly didn't want any bouncing baby mistakes, either. After all, she'd been one herself.

But it was slightly disconcerting to realize that she'd been completely lost in the heady heights of passion while Steve remained aware and prepared. "Have you ever forgotten?" she asked curiously. "Been so caught up in the heat of the moment that you either forgot or decided to risk it?"

"Never. I'm not stupid. I'm a risk-taker in some areas but not in that one." He eased her onto her back as he spoke, coming down on top of her. "And I've never been so *swept away* that I couldn't see the consequences looming before me."

"I just was," she whispered to herself. The hair on his chest felt wonderfully, sensually abrasive against her nipples. Steve was moving between her legs to make a place for himself there and she savored the full male pressure of his body. "With you. I—can't seem to think at all when you—when we—" Her voice trailed off and she gave a husky laugh. "I can't seem to talk, either."

"You have a similarly mind-blowing effect on me." His dark gaze locked with hers as his hands lifted her hips, positioning her to receive him.

Michelle felt him hard and hot against her and she inhaled sharply. She closed her eyes as he moved into her tight satin heat, pressing slowly, inexorably in. There was a sharp stab of pain as her body stretched to admit him and Michelle clamped her teeth down on her lip to keep from crying out. She could feel involuntary tears seep from the corners of her eyes.

And then he was deep inside her, full and hard. He lay there, breathing heavily, feeling her body adjust to accommodate him. "Ah, Michelle. You're so tight, so hot and sleek." He heaved a groan of pleasure. "You're perfect for me."

"Yes, I am," Michelle agreed throatily. "And not just in bed, either." The burning, stretching pain was slowly dissolving, giving way to a melting, dizzying pleasure.

He began to move and the pleasure swept through her in rhythmic waves, consuming and intimate and intense. The exquisite sensations radiating through her were like nothing she had ever experienced. Instinctively she moved in counterpoint to his rhythm, a passionate advance and retreat. Tension built and excitement soared, a rapturous heat shimmered through them, connecting them, bonding them, fierce and frantic and wild.

Michelle cried his name as the fever seared her, exploding her senses in a pleasure beyond description. Her body shuddered and clenched and she clung to Steve as the only anchor in a whirling, swirling sea of sensation.

Deep inside her, sheathed in ecstasy, Steve wanted to sustain the pleasure, but it was so immense, so intense, that Michelle's cries of completion and her sweet, inner contractions triggered his own shattering release.

And echoing in his head all through the pulsing climactic rapture was Michelle's husky, passionate avowal of love for him.

Eight

It was a long time before either of them surfaced, and even
after Steve had disengaged their bodies, Michelle lay cra-
dled in his arms, basking in the warm sensual afterglow.
They lay together silently. Only the noise of the traffic outside and an occasional thud in the living room—Burton
jumping on and off the furniture in pursuit of his mouse—
broke the stillness.

Michelle didn't mind the silence. She didn't need words,
she was too absorbed in her thoughts and her feelings to
talk. And her thoughts and feelings were all of Steve. How
much she loved him. How her love for him transcended the
sexual attraction between them and elevated the physical
pleasure they'd just shared. How it wasn't just sex between
them. It was love, the deep, true and abiding love she'd
wished and dreamed and prayed for all her life.

Steve was thinking, too, but his thoughts were not of true
love. His mind was replaying the sensual idyll that had just
transpired between them and this time he picked up certain

relevant, pertinent details he had missed while under the influence of the driving force of sexual hunger. And though it appeared that Michelle would be perfectly content to lie quietly, though his own blissfully drained body would prefer that, too, he knew there were certain things that could not be left unsaid.

"You're a virgin, aren't you?"

For a second or two, the question seemed to hang in the silence between them, until Michelle chirped brightly, "Not anymore."

She raised her head and grinned at him. She felt wonderful, filled with joy and love, vibrantly alive and deeply in love. She and Steve belonged together. It was elemental, natural and right. And so obvious; soon he would have to realize it, too.

The sunny warmth of her smile worked its magic on him. He was unable to sustain the emotional distance he'd been silently building—or any physical distance, either. He took her hand and lifted it to his mouth, kissing her palm. "You should have told me," he scolded mildly.

Michelle shrugged. "I didn't want to make a big deal out of it."

"Michelle, losing your virginity is a big deal."

She laughed, she couldn't help it. Sheer happiness was shimmering through her in radiant waves. "Some would say I was way overdue in losing mine." Emotional tears shone in her eyes as she gazed lovingly at him. "But I'm so glad I waited, Steve . . . that my first time was with you."

What could he say to that? What could he do but gather her even closer and kiss her until, astonishingly, he felt the stirrings of arousal again. *Again! After he'd just had her, he wanted her again!* That had certainly never happened to him before. After sex, he usually fell into a replete sleep or left the premises satiated, without any further need or desire for more contact. But then, his emotions had never been engaged before, not like now, the way they were with Michelle. They'd spent too much time together, their relationship was too layered, too complex for him to simply turn away from her.

But even this disconcerting evidence of his involvement didn't stop him from wrapping his arms around her and rolling onto his back, taking her with him so that she lay sprawled on top of him. Michelle laughed with delight, enjoying the sensual freedom this new position afforded her.

"I should be mad as hell at you for not telling me the truth," Steve said, sighing. "Not knowing...I could've hurt you, Michelle."

"But you didn't," she replied softly, feathering her lips along the strong line of his jaw. "You made it wonderful for me, Steve."

Steve caressed her, savoring the silky smooth texture of her skin. There was another reason why he should be furious with her, a far more selfish one. If giving one's virginity was a gift of love, then she'd made him the unwitting recipient of a gift he had never wanted. Had never asked for. He knew all about virgins and had always made it a point to avoid them. They came with too many strings attached, like love and promises, the ties that bind. Michelle had told him she loved him. Of course. To a twenty-five-year-old virgin, love and sex had to be irrevocably entwined.

Steve thought of his sister Jamie, the only other twenty-something virgin he had ever known. Rand Marshall, the man she'd finally allowed to take her to bed, had been a lot like Steve himself. A happy-go-lucky guy who liked women and good times, a guy in no hurry to give up his freedom and alter his fun and games life-style. Enter Jamie Saraceni and wham! Rand Marshall was hopelessly ensnared. Marriage and a baby had followed, fun and freedom had ended. Everytime Steve looked at his now thoroughly domesticated brother-in-law, he was struck with an acute case of schadenfreude.

And judging by the way he was carrying on with Michelle, the next time the wedding bells tolled, they would be tolling for him, Steve Saraceni.

Steve went hot, then cold, as if he were suffering fever and chills. Carefully he put Michelle away from him, and sat up.

"Steve?" She caressed his arm, her big blue eyes questioning. "Is there something wrong?"

"Wrong? What could possibly be wrong?" he replied in a voice filled with hearty faux cheer. "But it—it suddenly occurred to me that while we're lying here in your sister's bed, she might arrive at any moment. That could definitely be a bit awkward."

Michelle sat up, too, and leaned close to him, wrapping her arms around his waist and lying her head against the broad expanse of his back. "Don't worry. Courtney's out of town on some kind of investigative reporting assignment. She left the day after I got here. We have the place to ourselves."

"You've been staying here alone?" He turned around to face her. "Why?"

Michelle shrugged. There was no use rehashing the old birthday dinner quarrel. Today had changed so much between them. "I needed a vacation," she said lamely. "I've been doing all the sightseeing I never seem to do when Courtney's here." She tilted her head quizzically, suddenly remembering that she had no idea how he'd happened to show up at Courtney's door. "How did you know where I was?"

"I asked around," Steve mumbled.

"You did? But who did you ask? I didn't mention where I was going when I arranged for time off from work."

"I called Ashlinn in New York," Steve admitted grudgingly. "I thought maybe you were with her. You weren't, of course." He frowned. "Do we have to talk about this? Calling Ashlinn was hardly a pleasure, seeing as how she despises me. When I told her you'd left Harrisburg, she read me the riot act and refused to tell me where she thought you might be.''

"Oh dear." Michelle sighed. "That does sound like Ashlinn.''

"I had to call her three more times before she finally agreed to tell me that you might possibly be with Courtney in Washington. It took another two phone calls to get the address.''

"But you persisted." Michelle gave him a dazzling smile that almost stopped his heart. She was so beautiful she made him ache. "Oh, Steve, I'm so glad you did.''

Steve gave up his feeble attempts to withdraw from her. She was too tempting, too achingly near. The emotions surging through him were too powerful and too alluring to resist. He took her in his arms again.

"I'm glad, too," he said huskily. "I felt like a louse, canceling out on the dinner party Saturday night. Right after my family arrived, I called to invite you to join us." He grimaced, remembering. "I got your answering machine and that maddening, perky little message of yours." He proceeded to repeat her recorded message in its entirety.

"You've memorized it, word for word!" Michelle exclaimed, amazed.

"Because I heard it the forty times I called that night and another forty the next day. I probably used up the entire tape with my messages. Finally it was Monday and I called your office, only to hear that you'd taken some days off to go out of town.''

She gazed into the depths of his dark, dark eyes. "I wanted to get away for a little while, Steve.''

"Because I hurt you," he concluded, his expression regretful.

She nodded, then flashed him a grin. "You infuriated me, too. I felt as explosive as Three Mile Island.''

"I can relate to that. I went ballistic by the time I recorded message six hundred and twelve on your answering machine. Wait'll you hear."

They laughed, hugging, then tussling, then finally falling back on the mattress, their limbs entwined.

"Everything is going to be all right now," Michelle said breathlessly. "I know it."

Steve said nothing at all. He reached for his trusty packet, made use of it, and then watched her, his eyes glittering and intense, as he lifted her legs to his waist, then slowly sank into her.

Michelle gasped, expecting pain, but there was only a melting pliant heat as her body accepted him. He filled her again and again, her soft moans breaking the quiet darkness of the bedroom until her voice rose to a sharp cry and her body arched, tightening around his in an unmistakable climax.

And then he lost himself in her and the consuming, overwhelming whirlwind of their passion that merged them and made them one.

Back home again in Harrisburg, Michelle came to realize that everything had changed and yet nothing had changed between them. She and Steve saw each other as often as they had before her watershed trip to Washington, but now there was no more "chasing her around the room for a good night kiss." They ended every evening together in bed.

But no matter how late the hour Steve never stayed all night with her during the week, only on weekends, just for one night, never both. He maintained a need for his own time, space and freedom. Michelle soon recognized a pattern. After the times she and Steve had been exceptionally close, he would inevitably pull back, distancing himself from her, either physically or emotionally. Paradoxically she felt more insecure about her position in his life since they'd become intimate than before, when they were not.

Though she freely and often admitted her love for him—she couldn't *not* have told him, she loved him too much to hold back anything, even words—Steve did not reciprocate with his own declaration of love. He avoided any talk of the future. He didn't even make a date for more than a week in advance. Commitment? Permanence? Michelle was depressingly certain that those words weren't in his vocabulary. She suspected he'd probably even inked them out of his dictionary.

Still, they had certainly come a long way from the days when she hadn't even known which city he was in, Michelle reminded herself. And if it *looked* as if Steve was involved with her, if he *acted* as if he was committed to her by dating her exclusively, didn't it stand to reason that he actually was in love with her? Every time Michelle asked herself this question, she always came up with the same answer. Yes. Surely one of these days, Steve would, too.

May

"Michelle, can you believe it? The two of us playing golf at Hershey Country Club—what a hoot!" Leigh Wilson straightened the brim on her yellow golf hat, and grinned at Michelle through the ladies' locker room mirror.

Michelle surveyed her own image in the mirror. Her ecru-colored polo shirt and wide-cut taupe culottes, conservative in style and color, were certainly a far cry from the eye-catching, splashy golf clothes they'd seen in the pro shop of the club.

Leigh, all in yellow, looked like a bright canary, as she recombed her red hair and readjusted her hat for at least the fifth time. When she was finally satisfied, the two women headed for the first tee on the west course, where they were meeting the other half of their foursome, Steve Saraceni and Ed Dineen.

Steve was a member of the area's most exclusive club whose renowned golf course made invitations to play there highly prized indeed. The chance to play with a "scratch golfer" like Steve, who routinely shot par, was eagerly welcomed, as well.

Michelle had been present the morning Steve had invited Ed Dineen for a Saturday morning game of golf. Ed had accepted instantly, but to Michelle's surprise, Ed jettisoned Steve's proposal to invite two other legislators to join them.

"I have an idea, if you're game for something a little different," Ed said to Steve and, of course, Steve was more than willing to accommodate a legislator who might someday be voting on an issue crucial to one of Legislative Engineers Limited's clients.

"You see, no one has a better staff than I do," continued Ed, "and I like to reward—"

"I understand." Steve smiled that smooth as glass smile of his. "You want to invite Ken Gaudy and Jim Flinn to play golf with us." He named Dineen's top two aides. Familiarity with the legislators' staffs was extremely important to access and Steve knew them all.

"No." Ed shook his head. "Four guys on the golf course is commonplace, I said something *different!* How about we ask Michelle here and, uh, Leigh Wilson to play with us?"

"Play golf with Michelle and Leigh?" Steve's smile faltered. He didn't quite manage to conceal his dismay. Steve took his golf game very seriously, and his hours on the green did not include fledging amateurs, unless the said amateur happened to have a vote. Michelle and Leigh, junior staffers and female at that, most certainly did not.

"Have they ever played golf before?" Steve asked, catching Michelle's eye. He knew that she hadn't; she'd once told him so.

Michelle shrugged. It did seem an odd request for Ed to make.

"Who cares? We'll have a great time, no matter what!" Ed enthused.

Steve recovered himself enough to politely agree, though he'd complained about the arrangement to Michelle later that night as they lay together in bed.

"So you haven't picked up a golf club since you were twelve, and that was for miniature golf, hmm?" Steve groaned, looking martyred. "Well, I haven't played golf with a female since *I* was twelve and that was miniature golf with my kid sisters. Girls and golf just don't mix."

"Chauvinist!" Michelle playfully socked him. "Ed isn't a sexist, he's wonderfully egalitarian. That's why working for him is so rewarding."

"If you say so," grumbled Steve.

And so here they were, a foursome on the links. It was a beautiful day and Michelle was delighted to be able to spend this extra time with Steve. He patiently showed her which club to use, how to hold and swing it. She loved having his arms around her during the lessons. The long hard length of his body surrounding hers was exciting and evocative; learning to swing the club couldn't compare to the thrill of being in his arms . . .

Michelle was so absorbed in Steve that it took her longer than usual to notice that while Steve was tutoring her in the fine points of golf, Ed had taken on the task of instructing Leigh in much the same way. Ed's arms encircled Leigh, their bodies pressed close, moving in sync as they swung the club. Soon, the two of them, laughing and talking and re-taking countless practice shots, were lagging far behind Steve and Michelle.

Steve glanced impatiently at his watch. "The foursome behind us must be ready to twist their nine irons around our necks," he gritted, watching the other couple's antics.

Michelle said nothing, out of loyalty to her boss. She couldn't admit, not even to Steve, that she found Ed's behavior—well, embarrassing. And oddly disappointing, too.

It was the first time she had ever found reason to question anything the senator did. But why was he acting so uncharacteristically *silly* with Leigh?

Finally, finally, they were on the eighteenth hole and in sight of the clubhouse. Michelle and Steve finished first, then waited for Ed and Leigh to join them. "What a day!" Steve grimaced. "I feel like we were on a double date with Ken and Barbie." He reached over to catch Michelle's hand. "On the positive side, you weren't bad for a beginner, Michelle. With some lessons and enough practice, you'd be an okay player."

"High praise indeed," Michelle said dryly.

When Steve suggested treating everybody to lunch, Ed immediately accepted. "Steve, didn't I tell you this would be fun?" Ed demanded jovially. "What do you say we do it again, real soon?"

Michelle almost laughed out loud at Steve's horrified expression, one he quickly managed to mask. "Sure, Ed. We'll have to do it again," he replied with commendable sincerity.

"When hell freezes over," Steve amended privately to Michelle as they walked toward the clubhouse. Ed and Leigh were lollygagging behind, as giddy as a pair of high school students playing hooky on a warm spring day.

"It's an unwritten rule that a guy doesn't carry on his flings on the golf course," Steve added, casting a critical glance at the other couple.

"Ed isn't having a fling with Leigh!" Michelle exclaimed, aghast at the very mention of such an unbelievable prospect. "I admit he has been acting unlike his usual self." She gulped. "But he would never be unfaithful to his wife. He's a devoted family man. His old-fashioned values are part and parcel of his appeal."

Agitated, she caught Steve's arm. "I know this is the way gossip starts. People see a senator and a staff member together out of the office, laughing and having a good time, and assume the worst. But—''

"You mean, they assume the obvious," Steve said wryly. "Which is generally right on the mark."

"Not Ed!" Michelle insisted. "There has never been any scandal attached to Ed's name. He's not a womanizer and Valerie would be so hurt if she were to hear—rumors. Please, Steve, promise me you won't, well, mention anything about Ed and Leigh and—and this afternoon."

Michelle was well aware of the efficiency of the Harrisburg grapevine. It relayed gossip, innuendos and rumors faster than any electronic communications system. And lobbyists were renowned contributors. If Steve alluded to Ed Dineen's flirtatious behavior with a female staffer—on the golf course of the Hershey Country Club!—the tale would spread like wildfire, with various titillating embellishments added to each retelling.

"I won't say a word," Steve promised, but he stared at Michelle with troubled dark eyes. "Michelle, you don't believe all Dineen's press clippings, do you? Keep in mind that you've written some of them yourself. What the voting public is told about a politician is often a far cry from the type of man he really is."

"Maybe in some cases," Michelle conceded. "But I couldn't work behind a sham. I have to believe in the people I work for and with. Ed and Valerie Dineen are—''

"You're not cynical enough, Michelle," Steve cut in. "You haven't developed the hard shell you need to weather the hypocrisies and necessary compromises of politics. I worry about you," he added gruffly. "I don't want to see you get hurt, and you will be, if Dineen doesn't live up to your high expectations of him."

He realized at that moment how very much he didn't want her to be hurt. He knew he would protect her—if he could.

Michelle gazed at Steve thoughtfully. He really did seem concerned for her. Taking encouragement from that, she

decided to brave asking him what she had not yet dared to
ask. "Steve, Courtney called me last week to tell me that
she's getting married next weekend," she said in a rush.
"The wedding is going to be very small, only family, and
unfortunately, not everybody can make it to Washington on
such short notice. But Courtney said I could bring a guest.
Would you like to go with me?"

"Next weekend?" Steve stalled for time. Over the years
he'd attended more weddings than he could count, and that
included serving as a groomsman in quite a few. He had an
ironclad rule about weddings, though. Always go alone.
Taking a date to such an emotional, symbol-laden event was
like taking a stroll through a mine field. Unless one thrived
on potential disaster, both were best avoided. As for taking
Michelle to a private family wedding...

He felt himself beginning to sweat, though there was no
external reason for it. He'd had a refreshing shower in the
locker room and the day was sunny, but not hot. The heat
he was feeling was strictly internal.

"Next weekend is bad for me," he heard himself saying.
"I'm booked solid—with golf games here at the club with
half the state senate. I'm sorry, honey."

"I thought that was probably the case." Michelle masked
her disappointment well. "But I thought—well, there's no
harm in asking."

Steve was inordinately relieved by her uncomplaining ac-
ceptance. "No harm at all."

Michelle had just freed Squeaky and Burton from their
respective cat carriers—this time both cats had made the trip
to Washington with her—when the phone rang.

"You're back!" Steve greeted her exuberantly before
she'd even said hello. "It's about time, too. I've been calling all day. How was the wedding?"

She was surprised at his unbridled enthusiasm. Nor had
she expected to hear from him tonight. He'd been aloof and

detached every time she'd mentioned the wedding. Though she had accepted his "booked solid" excuse, Michelle was well aware that, to Steve, escorting her to her sister's wedding, was as appealing as radiation poisoning.

"The wedding was lovely," she said quietly. "Courtney was beautiful, Connor was handsome and little Sarah, the baby they're adopting, was good as gold all through the ceremony."

"Good. I'm glad everything worked out for them. Can I come over?"

"Now? Tonight?" Michelle's heart skipped a beat. All during the drive home she'd been hoping to see him tonight but she'd also recognized the possibility that she might not, depending on his schedule—or his particular whims. As much as she loved him, as close as they were at times, she still wasn't entirely sure of him. Sometimes she wondered if she ever would be.

"Now, tonight," Steve repeated affirmatively. "If I leave my place right now, I'll be there within fifteen minutes, maybe less if the traffic's light."

Could he actually have missed her? Michelle wondered, and hope soared within her. Watching Courtney and Connor together this weekend had filled her with powerful longings for a wedding of her own. Which was probably why Steve had opted out of attending the ceremony, she mused grimly. A man as experienced as he would expect such behavior from a woman. But the fact remained—she wanted to marry Steve, not to date him.

Steve arrived, buoyant and vibrant, as high spirited as she'd ever seen him. He gifted the cats with two of the tiny furry toy mice they adored, then presented Michelle with a gift-wrapped box from an exclusive lingerie boutique.

But she didn't get a chance to open it, for he swept her up in his arms and carried her off to the bedroom. He was on top of the world, the Viking warrior snatching the prettiest wench in the village, the bold knight claiming his fair maiden, the lobbyist with a guarantee that the bill affecting his client would easily pass both state houses during Tuesday morning's session, granting him a big, big bonus. And he was here with his sweet and sexy lover.

"I think you missed me," Michelle whispered as he swiftly, deftly removed her teal blue camp shirt and shorts. She was wearing a lacy teddy in a matching shade of teal under it. When she'd put it on, she'd dreamed of him seeing her in it—and removing it.

Which he did with relish. "I did miss you," he admitted, cupping her breasts. A surge of emotion swept through him, stunning him with its force. It occurred to him that he really had missed her this weekend. Desperately. Alarmingly. But he was *not* getting dependent on her, he swore to himself.

"I'm not used to spending weekends on my own," Steve clarified his admission, his voice raspy with passion. His hands glided possessively over the curves of her waist, her hips, her thighs. "I'm not used to going nearly three entire days without sex."

"Poor, poor Steve." Michelle helped him pull off his clothes, her hands trembling as she touched the warmth of his skin, the hardness of his muscles. "We'll have to make up for all that lost time, won't we?"

He muttered an unintelligible exclamation and pulled her into his arms for a deep, hungry kiss, devastating in its intensity. Without breaking the kiss, he lowered her to the bed, slipping his thigh between her legs. Pliant and yearning, Michelle arched her body into the hard warmth of his.

During the weekend apart, both had thought constantly of each other, hungered for each other, and now that they were together, they were primed and ready for the rapturous pleasure and release they always found in each other's arms.

"Steve, love me now," cried Michelle, clinging to him, wanting him with a fervid need that was elemental and profound and almost painful in its intensity.

"Yes, baby." With a low, sexy sound, he did just that, filling her, making her moan as their bodies moved together in a timeless rhythm that was universal yet uniquely their own. Passion and urgency swept them into a vortex of wild, mindless pleasure that built and grew and finally exploded into a burst of sensual rapture.

Languid and mellow in the sweet aftermath, Michelle cuddled close and kissed him lightly, lovingly. "I love you, Steve."

It was only much later, after he'd awakened at dawn, that Steve realized a certain, shocking omission, the first one of his life. He'd been in such an all-fired hurry to get over here to Michelle that he'd forgotten all about taking precautions. He'd completely forgotten the vital step that for years had ensured him freedom and peace of mind.

Surprisingly he didn't go rigid with horror. He was feeling far too confident to worry about a single lapse. Everything was going his way. He was on a career high and his personal life was deeper, richer, more satisfying than ever before.

Steve gazed down at Michelle, sleeping soundly on her back, her lips slightly parted, her lovely face completely relaxed in repose. He couldn't bring himself to leave her tonight and return to his own place to spend the night, as he usually did. He smiled, remembering how thrilled she'd been that he had agreed to spend the night. He really should do it more often, he decided. He liked sleeping with her, literally sleeping. But not as much as he enjoyed making love to her. He wanted her again, in the most urgent way. Steve paused for only a moment before reaching for her.

A single lapse. Well, he was feeling lucky now. In retrospect, when had he ever not been lucky? He expected things to go well for him and they inevitably did. Wanting Michelle as much as he did, he could certainly risk a double lapse. Besides, he couldn't *not* make love to Michelle. He had been able to turn away from women in the past if and when he chose, but tonight, right now, there was no choice to make. It was as if he and Michelle were destined to make love, and within a few passionate moments, they were experiencing the same desperate passion all over again.

Nine

July 4

It was now or never. Steve surveyed the members of the extended Saraceni clan, plus assorted friends and neighbors, gathered in the backyard of his parents' Merlton, New Jersey, home. The yard was much too small to accommodate all the guests who spilled boisterously into the house and front yard. People juggled their plates and their drinks while they ate, standing or sitting on the grass.

Because he was a glamorous out-of-towner, as well as the adored eldest and only son, Steve was always assured a place at the sturdy, polished picnic table that his father had crafted years ago. Steve toyed with his ravioli—handmade by his grandmother because what would the Fourth of July be without Grandma's ravioli?—then laid down his fork, his expression grimly determined.

He stood up, raised his voice to deep-pitched resonance and said, "I have an announcement to make." A respectful hush fell over the crowd. When Steve Saraceni spoke, his adoring family and friends listened. Steve cleared his throat. "I'm getting married," he announced.

There was a momentary stunned silence, and then pandemonium erupted. His mother and aunts began to cry joyful tears, his father and uncles rushed to shake his hand and jovially slap his back. His grandmother caught him in a bear hug whose force left him winded despite her diminutive size. Steve answered his well-wishers questions with his usual suavity, smiling and joking, rather enjoying being the center of such enthusiastic, ebullient attention.

Until he happened to catch a glimpse of his sister Jamie. She was standing a few feet away from him, apart from his crowd of admirers and watching him, her face devoid of expression. But her big dark eyes were flashing and Steve read the message in them. Jamie wasn't buying it, not at all, and that one look from her sent him plunging painfully back to reality. Depressing, painful reality.

Getting married? Michelle hated his guts! She thought he'd used her to gain confidential information. He had made her pregnant, and she'd left town after telling him she never wanted to see him again.

An hour later, needing a breather from the pressing adulation, Steve slipped upstairs to seek refuge in his old bedroom. It was exactly as he'd left it when he had permanently moved out after college, a sort of shrine to his boyhood and adolescence. His sister Jamie was in there, diapering her nearly seven-month-old son, Matthew, on the bed. Steve tried to unobtrusively back out. The last person he wanted to talk to was—

"What are you up to now, Steve Saraceni?" Jamie's voice, stern and disapproving, caught him before he could make his escape.

He managed a sickly smile. "I guess you're as surprised as everybody else about my, uh, uh, big news, eh, Jame?"

"I don't believe a word of it," Jamie said flatly. "I don't know what's going on with you but you've sunk to new depths this time, dragging the entire family into your latest devious scheme. Didn't it ever occur to you that Mom and Dad and Grandma have been living for the day when you finally get married? That they're going to be hurt and disappointed when—"

"Didn't it ever occur to you that I might be telling the truth?" Steve snapped. Jamie's condemnatory harangues had always irritated him, never more so than now. "That maybe I really am getting married?"

"No. I seemed to be the only one who noticed the very conspicuous absence of the bride-to-be." Jamie scowled at him, dark eyes snapping. "Oh, sure, you explained that she's visiting her family. That just doesn't ring true, Steve. If you, of all people, really were engaged you'd have your fiancée with you when you made the announcement, and don't tell me how I know that, I just do. I know you, Steve. Very, very well. So whatever this nasty little plot you've concocted is about—"

"Okay, okay. Maybe I was a bit, er, premature with my announcement." Steve's defenses crumpled. He sat down on the bed and gazed blindly at his small nephew who was sucking vigorously on a pacifier. The baby had a shock of straight, dark hair and gazed up at Steve with his huge dark eyes, so like his mother's, so like his uncle's, then grinned widely around the pacifier.

"He's a charmer." Steve touched the baby's small, sturdy fist.

"Mom and Grandma tell me constantly that he looks exactly like you did as a baby. I can understand why they doted on you so," Jamie said dryly. She picked up little Matthew, smiling at him and cuddling him close. "But heaven help us, Rand and I aren't going to spoil Matthew the way you've been spoiled, Steve. All your life you've gotten what you wanted by—"

"Your baby is so cute, Jamie," Steve interrupted distractedly, awestruck by the child's appeal. Little Matthew was laughing over his mother's shoulder. When the pacifier dropped out of his mouth, he emitted a loud sound of baby protest, then began to chuckle again. Steve couldn't take his eyes off him. "Why, he's adorable! And he's obviously smart and—"

"Cassie's boys were just as cute and sweet as Matthew as babies," Jamie cut in loyally. "You just never glanced their way until they turned five and could talk about TV shows and video games with you."

Steve swallowed. "I've changed, Jamie. I'm different from the guy you've known—and disapproved of—all these years."

Why, it was true! Steve was thunderstruck by the revelation. Though he hadn't fully realized it until this moment, he really had changed! The simple fact that he'd dated Michelle exclusively—and been faithful to her for the past six months—was proof enough. But the changes within him, as their relationship deepened and evolved, had been so gradual and so natural, that he hadn't even been aware of them. Until now.

"You claim you've changed." Jamie eyed him skeptically. "And now you expect me to believe that you're seriously interested in marriage and babies?"

Steve nodded with all the verve and vigor of a true believer. And now that he'd decided on his course of action, marrying Michelle, he would pull out all stops to achieve his ends. Convincing the dubious Jamie seemed a necessary prelude in winning back Michelle. He smiled his most effective, heart-melting smile. "Jamie, do you think if I had a, um, a baby, he would look like your little Matthew? I really hope so, although a little blue-eyed blonde would certainly be nice, too.''

Jamie's heart appeared to remain unmelted. She did, however, gasp with shock and sink down onto the bed, the baby wriggling in her arms. "Holy saints!" she exclaimed, sounding a lot like Grandma. "Now I get it! You're going to be a father! This woman, this Michelle, the one you say you're going to marry, the one Saran told us you'd been seeing quite a lot of.... She's pregnant, isn't she, Steve?"

Steve's smile dissolved. A hideous lump of what felt like ground glass swelled in his throat and he couldn't make a sound, only nod his head.

"Oh, Steve, how could you? Poor Michelle! No wonder she's not here. When she told you the news, you told her it was her tough luck, didn't you? You told her to get lost!"

"No, no! You've got it all wrong!" Steve stood up and began to agitatedly pace the room. "I didn't say any of those things, Jamie. I made a date to see her at dinner to talk things out but she was gone when I arrived at her place. I tried to contact her. I called her stepsister who lives in New York but only got the answering machine and I don't know where the stepsister in D.C. lives since her marriage in May so I—"

"Did you ask Michelle to marry you when she told you she was pregnant?" Jamie demanded. "Did you tell her you loved her and that you were happy she was carrying your child?"

Steve blanched. "No. I—I was shocked, Jamie. I never expected—"

"You are such a snake!" Jamie raged. She stood up and began to pace, too. "You aren't careful and then you have the nerve to be shocked by the natural consequences! You didn't say what that poor girl desperately needed to hear, and now you have the nerve to whine that she ran out on you."

Jamie snatched a magazine from the nightstand, rolled it up and began whacking Steve with it. Matthew waved his chubby little arms and chimed in vociferously with his own baby syllables.

"Hey, what's this? The latest sortie in Saraceni sibling warfare?" Rand Marshall, Jamie's husband, entered the room and took in the scene at a glance. Baby Matthew crowed with delight at the sight of Rand and launched himself into his father's arms. "Stop picking on poor Steve, Jamie," Rand added drolly. "After all, he's only twice your size."

Jamie dropped the magazine but her dark eyes were glittering with emotion. "Oh, Rand, he's really done it this time. He got a girl pregnant and rejected her and now he's telling the family he intends to marry her when he doesn't."

"But I do!" Steve exclaimed. "I really want to marry her. After I made the announcement to the family, I—I realized that I wanted it to be true. And having to defend myself to you totally convinced me, Jamie. I *want* to marry Michelle."

"Do you love her?" Rand asked wryly.

"Yes." Steve's dark eyes were filled with pain. It was the first time he had admitted it, even to himself. If only Michelle had been around to hear it. "I love her. More than I wanted to. I never wanted to fall in love. But it happened and I want her forever. I'll never be happy without her, I know that now."

"Why don't you tell her so?" suggested Rand.

"Only leave out all the I-never-wanted-to-love-you angst," Jamie added. "Instead, say that you—"

"Honey, you don't have to write a script for him," Rand said amusedly. "When it comes to making a case for himself, your brother is in a class all his own."

"Not this time." Dispirited, Steve sat down in his old desk chair. "You see, there's an additional complication. Michelle thinks I used her to obtain inside information for one of my clients about a bill her boss introduced.''

"Did you?'' Jamie asked severely.

Steve winced. "No. I had some confidential inside information, but not from Michelle. I learned where the sites being considered for hazardous waste elimination centers by the committee were to be located and passed on the word to my client. They bought property in the proposed counties. When the bill passed, they were right there, as owners of the land.''

"So your clients got the contracts to build the centers, you got a nice fat bonus, but Michelle ended up pregnant, feeling used and abandoned.'' Jamie shook her head. "There's no easy way out of this one, brother dear.'' Rather tentatively, she patted his arm. "For the first time in our lives, I actually feel sorry for you. And if you really love Michelle, I hope she'll give you another chance to prove it.''

"I really do,'' Steve said. The familiar steely glint of determination glittered in his dark eyes. "And she will. The next time I'm in Merlton, Michelle will be with me—as my wife.''

It was hot and muggy when Michelle pulled her car into the parking lot adjacent to her apartment building. The drive from Washington had taken longer than usual due to the heavy holiday weekend traffic and Burton and Squeaky, secure in their cat carriers, were not at all pleased with their temporary captivity. Michelle had to play the radio extra loud to drown out their incessant meowing complaints, and her ears were ringing as she climbed out of the car.

She was relieved to be home. Her holiday visit to Courtney and Connor had been a mistake. All weekend long, as she'd watched the newlyweds so deeply in love with each other, the weight of her own loneliness had grown to crushing proportions. The man she loved hadn't loved her at all.

He'd used her, to obtain information about *hazardous waste elimination sites*. It was galling, it was heartbreaking—it was downright toxic! Fury momentarily supplanted her despair.

But only momentarily. Michelle's thoughts rarely strayed from the new little life growing within her and soon shifted back to her pregnancy. This past weekend she'd been acutely aware of three-month-old Sarah and the constant care and attention that an infant required. Lucky little Sarah had two devoted parents to care for her, a stay-at-home mother and a hands-on daddy who willingly pitched in to help whenever he was home.

The family interaction had been wonderful as well as painful for Michelle to watch, underscoring the practicalities of her own predicament. Who was going to be there for *her* baby twenty-four hours a day? She would have to work full-time as there would be no husband to support them. And there would be no daddy to take over for a tired mother or to share the pleasures and the anxieties and all the little details of parenthood.

Michelle reached into the back seat to remove the cats from the car. She felt like crying. She'd been doing a lot of that lately, although only at night, alone in bed in the dark. She wasn't ready to share her secret just yet, she wasn't ready to admit that she'd been *Hooked!* just like those hapless, heartbroken women in Ashlinn's proposed book.

"Let me get those for you."

Michelle jumped at the sound. She recognized Steve's voice, of course, without turning around. "Don't bother," she said coldly, hanging onto the handles of the cat carriers, one in each hand.

"I insist." He reached for them, touching her in the process.

Michelle instantly set the carriers on the ground. His touch, impersonal and serviceable as it was, was too much for her to cope with. Grimacing, she reached for her suitcase.

"Leave it," Steve ordered, picking up the cats. "I'll come back for it."

"No thank you. I can manage." The bag wasn't heavy and she easily lifted it. Her heart was pounding, her stomach as jumpy as a restless, caged cat, but she hid her anxiety behind a coolly impenetrable facade. Silently she headed into her apartment; Steve following close behind.

As tempting as it was, she couldn't slam the door in his face, leaving him outside. He had her cats, guaranteeing him entry. Which was exactly what he'd planned, of course. Michelle scowled. Steve Saraceni always had a plan, one he would successfully implement to suit his own ends. No one knew that better than she.

Once inside, Steve freed the cats, then stood watching her, his dark eyes sharp and intent. "I have a whole carload of gifts in my car for you," he said at last. "I went to a mall while I was in Jersey and for the first time ever, I ended up buying more than my shop-aholic cousin Saran. I bought you perfume, candy, books, silk flowers, lingerie. Oh, and a life-size toy cat that looks so real Burt and Squeak will either try to fight it or adopt it. If I go down to my car to get the stuff, will you let me back inside?"

"No," Michelle said succinctly, her blue eyes as icy as her tone.

"I figured you wouldn't. That's why I didn't try." He sat down on the sofa, stretching one arm along the back of it, lifting his right ankle to rest upon his left knee, casual and relaxed, as if he were settling down to watch some TV. Only his eyes, intense and piercing, belied his carefree mode.

For a while Michelle pretended he wasn't there. She put food down for the cats, unpacked her bags and straightened up the already orderly living room. Finally the strain of his watchful presence was too much for her.

"You can leave anytime," she said caustically. "The sooner the better."

"I'm not leaving, Michelle."

"Well, you certainly aren't staying."

"Yes," Steve said calmly. "I am."

"You can't!" Michelle stared at him. It occurred to her that if he refused to leave, she had no means of forcibly evicting him from the premises. He was bigger and stronger than her in every way. She couldn't physically pick him up and toss him out the door. Frustration roiled within her. "If you're trying to infuriate me, you're succeeding masterfully." She clenched her teeth tightly. "I suppose there's a reason you're inflicting yourself on me. Say what it is and then get out!"

"I want to marry you," Steve said bluntly.

Whatever she'd been expecting him to say, it hadn't been that! She was unprepared, tired and vulnerable. Unexpected, unwelcome emotional tears filled her eyes. She tried to blink them away. "Just drop the euphemisms and say what you really mean for once. You don't *want* to marry me, you feel obligated to make the offer. Well, don't do me any favors, Steve. I don't want to marry you, either."

"Yes, you do," Steve said calmly. "So let's get married, Michelle. As soon as possible. If we apply for the license tomorrow, we can be married by the end of the week."

He made it sound so easy, so logical. Michelle was incensed. "Don't insult my intelligence! You're the man who wouldn't even attend my sister's wedding with me and now I'm supposed to believe that you want to be *in* one with me? I know all about your aversion to marriage and commitment, remember? You told me countless times how much your freedom means to you."

"That was when I was confusing narcissism with freedom," Steve said. "I'm not, not anymore."

"Where did you come up with *that?*"

He shrugged sheepishly. "My sister Jamie. But she was right on target, I can see that now."

"Well, I can't. If I hadn't been stupid enough to go to your office and tell you about—" Michelle swallowed "—that I'm pregnant, you never would've bothered to see me again. After all, I'd served my purpose to you. You found out where the committee voted to place the hazardous waste sites and relayed the news to your client. You got a big cash bonus for your efforts and you—"

"I intend to use that bonus as a down payment on a house for us. I've arranged for a realtor to take us around to look at places later in the week."

Michelle was outraged. "When it comes to—to sheer audacity and tenacity, you have no equal! I don't know why you're even going through this charade. You don't care about me!"

"Yes, I do." Steve stood up. "And I'll prove it to you. I can refute your arguments point by point. First—"

"Stop trying to lobby me!"

"I'm not lobbying you, I'm trying to tell you that I love you!" His voice rose. His first proposal and he was botching it. His lobbying skills suggested backing off and trying a new angle, but he wasn't a lobbyist now, he was a man in love.

Passionately, Steve forged ahead. "Michelle, you were *not* stupid to tell me you're pregnant. But even if you hadn't come to my office last week, I would've found out anyway because I certainly intended to see you again. I would've called you, sweetheart. I missed you and—"

"If this wasn't so nauseating, it would be hilarious," Michelle cut in crossly. "Steven Saraceni's revisionist relationship history—conveniently ignore the facts and make up new ones. The truth is that you hadn't called me for two and a half weeks after our fight. It was definitely all over between us."

"It wasn't over, although that was the worst fight we'd ever had. Actually, it was our only serious quarrel, which certainly proves how strong our compatibility quotient really is. But think back to that fight, Michelle. You accused me of using you to gain information. You said I deliberately sought you out because of your position on the committee, that I was a back-stabbing double-crosser because I took advantage of your feelings for me to use for my own political gains. You didn't believe me when I denied it, you'd already tried, judged and found me guilty. I was furious, Michelle. I was also hurt that you had so little faith or trust in me. I—" Steve cleared his throat and looked at the floor. "I kept expecting you to call me to apologize."

"*Me* apologize to *you?*" she echoed incredulously.

He nodded. "I respected everything you ever told me as a confidence between us, Michelle. I never used you. But you wouldn't believe me."

She folded her arms in front of her chest and glared at him. "I still don't believe you. I remember how quick you were to use the information I gave you about Ed's basketball career way back in January. You spotted me as a...a source and cultivated our relationship and I was naive enough to trust you and confide in you. But it's my fault, too. I should have known it would end badly. I received a chain letter the day I met you, promising doom and destruction if I broke the chain. Well, I did break it, and look what happened to me. *You!*"

"Michelle, the day we met was the luckiest day of my life, and these past months have been the happiest. You fell in love with me and I...fell in love with you, too." He walked toward her. "I want you and I want our baby, sweetheart."

The closer he came, the faster Michelle's bravado faded. He held out his hand to her and she refused it, backing away from him. "Don't touch me! And stop lying to me! You don't love me and you never have. You saw my love as a weakness and since you're a man who exploits other people's weaknesses, you used me and my love for you. You used me politically and sexually and when you were finished with me, you were perfectly content to end it between us."

Her temples were beginning to throb from the tension and she rubbed them with her fingertips. "But you must've had second thoughts about my pregnancy," she continued grimly. "Enough people have seen us together these past months to connect you with this baby I'm having and you've decided that the politically correct thing to do is to marry me and avoid gossip.

"Well, that's not enough for me, Steve." Her voice rose, straining with emotion. "I've been in this situation before, you know, twenty-five years ago when *I* was the baby who caused two people to live unhappily in a miserable marriage. I won't put my child in that position. And I won't make someone else a prisoner in a marriage he doesn't want." To her horror, she nearly burst into tears.

Steve tried to take her into his arms, but she pushed him away. If there had been a magazine handy, she probably would've rolled it up and started smacking him with it, he acknowledged gloomily. Jamie was right—this wasn't going to be easy. But he was not giving up!

"There isn't going to be a divorce, Michelle. When I marry, it's for life, and I fully intend for our marriage to be as happy and successful as my parents' marriage has been all these years." He stared at her, his face lighting in a sudden illuminating smile.

"This must be one of those cataclysmic moments of truth that always seem to happen to other people. But now it's happening to me. *I want to be happily married to the woman I love.* That's why I waited all these years, playing the field, taking my time. I was waiting for you, Michelle, the one woman I could truly love for the rest of my life. The reason I avoided marriage in the past is because I'm so serious about it. I avoided commitment because I'm deeply committed to it. But now I have you and I want to commit myself to you, Michelle. I want to marry you, my darling.''

It was the most impassioned and sincere speech of his life and he felt paradoxically drained and exhilarated. He waited for her to run into his arms. Then he could pick her up and carry her to bed and demonstrate his intentions and his love physically, just as he'd done verbally. That was what was supposed to happen after a guy bared his soul to the woman he loved. Wasn't it?

Apparently not. Michelle's face didn't soften with love, she didn't run into his arms. She laughed. And not happily, not joyfully. Her laughter was unmistakably derisive—and filled with disbelief.

''You're amazing, Steve. No one can twist things around to serve your own ends like you can. You can take facts and turn them into fiction like a magician changes a handkerchief into a canary. You don't make 180 degree turns; yours are more like 540 degrees, but you manage to seem credible anyway.''

Steve's lips thinned into a straight line and his eyes narrowed to slits. She'd just thrown his declaration of love and his proposal back in his face! Anger surged through him, mixed by a terrible hurt at the injustice of it all.

''If you're trying to infuriate me, you're succeeding *masterfully,*'' he said in a taut, controlled voice, deliberately using her own words. ''If you're trying to hurt me, you've accomplished that, too. I'll take whatever you dish out because I deserve it for getting you pregnant. You have every right to be furious with me and I don't blame you for thinking that you hate my guts. But I can only take it in small doses and I've had enough tonight, Michelle. I'll leave you now, since you so obviously want me to.''

He strode to the door, carefully sidestepping Squeaky who was chasing after a tiny spongy ball. He didn't look back and he didn't say goodbye.

After he'd gone, Michelle stood staring at the closed door. She should be pleased with herself, she'd driven him away. That had been her aim, hadn't it? Steve Saraceni was very clever at taking pipe dreams and making them seem real and she wasn't about to succumb to his skills again. No matter how desperately she might want to.

Ten

Michelle was keenly aware that the atmosphere in Ed Dineen's office on Monday morning was curiously, uncharacteristically somber. There were none of the usual half-joking moans and groans about the iniquities of facing a Monday morning, no swapping tales about the holiday weekend. If anyone spoke at all it was in hushed, funereal tones. Was she in an office or a morgue? Michelle mused. She remarked on the radical change to Brendan O'Neal when he came into her office with her mail.

"You mean you haven't heard?" Brendan was astonished. "Where have you been, locked up in a monastery in Katmandu? I thought everybody in Harrisburg would've heard by now. The reason we're all in such a funk is because Ed and Valerie Dineen have split up."

Michelle felt as if she'd been socked in the solar plexus. "No!" It was more a pained denial than an exclamation. She gripped the edge of her desk. "When? *Why?*"

"Ed made the announcement on Friday," Brendan said grimly. "He left Valerie and the children for— Want me to quote him? Hold on to your stomach, this is going to make you gag—'the most exciting woman in the world, the one who makes him feel like a man in ways he never dreamed possible.'"

"Stop." Michelle weakly held up her hand. "You're right, I am going to gag. Brendan, please tell me you're making a very bad joke. Ed couldn't have said that, he couldn't have done that!"

"Oh, it gets worse. Do you know who this career-ending, home-wrecker is, Michelle? None other than our very own Leigh Wilson. Apparently she and Ed have been carrying on all over town for the past couple months. They weren't very discreet, either, according to everybody I've talked to, although all of us here in Ed's office and poor Valerie must've been wearing blinders. We were literally the last ones to find out."

"Ed and Leigh?" Michelle lost her grip on the desk and slid numbly into her chair. "Oh, Brendan, it can't be true!"

"It is," Brendan said bluntly. He eyed her curiously. "I'm surprised you didn't know, Michelle. I mean, Saraceni knew—every lobbyist in town did. Rumor has it that Saraceni, Lassiter, Exner, and three NEA lobbyists actually caught Ed and Leigh in, er, flagrante delicto at an NEA fund-raiser one night."

Michelle gaped at him, speechless.

"Joe McClusky's staff has been telling everybody that Ed's been handing out confidential information like campaign buttons, hoping to buy himself some goodwill and secrecy," Brendan continued glumly. His expression, his posture and tone conveyed total demoralization. "It didn't work, of course. The inside tips Ed gave out have fueled even more gossip. He's shown such horrible judgment, Michelle. I can't help but wonder if Ed Dineen ever was who we all thought he was or just a grandstanding actor playing a role while it suited him, then getting bored with it and shucking the whole show.''

Michelle stared at the smooth surface of her desk. "It was Ed who told Steve the location of the sites for the hazardous waste elimination centers," she said softly. She knew it now with blinding certainty.

"Undoubtedly," agreed Brendan.

Michelle flinched as everything fell into place with ferocious precision. She had been certain that she herself must've unthinkingly told Steve about the sites and that he had used the information to his client's benefit. After all, she confided in him about everything and anything. Wasn't it obvious to assume that she was the leak?

Michelle's face burned. Steve had admitted having the information but denied getting it from her. And she had accused him of being a liar as well as a back-stabbing double-crosser.

But he was neither. Steve had received that information directly from Ed and had used it without compunction. There had been betrayal, but not from her. Ed Dineen had betrayed his wife and his staff and his constituents. And she had betrayed Steve by her appalling lack of faith in him.

Michelle stood up, her legs so shaky she felt as if she were walking on rubber. "Brendan, I—I'm going out." She grabbed her purse and headed out of the office.

She walked directly to Steve's office, a few blocks away. She was perspiring from the summer heat and panting from her brisk pace when she entered the office suite of Legislative Engineers Limited.

"Oh, hi!" called Steve's cousin Saran, who was sitting at the reception desk filing her astonishingly long, pointed fingernails. "I don't know how you nailed him, but congratulations!"

"Nailed him?" Michelle echoed faintly.

Saran grinned. "Too bad you weren't with Steve in Merlton when he made *the big announcement*. Wow, everybody just went crazy! So when's the wedding? Is it going to be big, like Jamie's wedding was? She invited half the world, I think. I can't picture Steve in a scene like that, but hey, I couldn't picture him getting married, either. I'm really excited for you both."

Michelle stared at Saran, comprehension slowly dawning. Steve had told his family that he was marrying her? She began to tremble.

"Want me to buzz Steve and tell him that you're here or are you going to, like, romantically surprise him?" asked Saran.

"Don't tell him I'm here," Michelle said quickly. That way he couldn't say he didn't want to see her. Not that she could blame him if he didn't. When she thought about the things she'd said to him, the hateful, hurtful things that were all untrue....

If Saran hadn't been watching expectantly, waiting for her to go in and "romantically surprise" Steve with her appearance, Michelle knew she would have bolted. As it was, she walked slowly back to Steve's office and quietly opened his door. He was sitting at his desk, talking on the phone. Michelle froze, her hand on the knob.

Steve glanced up and their eyes connected. And held. "Can I call you back, Don?" Michelle heard him say. She stood in the doorway, her heart thundering in her ears as Steve hung up the phone.

She was struck by a walloping case of déjà vu. Just last week she had come to this office, feeling as scared and uncertain as she felt now, to inform Steve of her pregnancy. She'd certainly made a mess of that. What if she blundered now, again? Yesterday he had bared his heart and soul for her and she had laughed and sent him away. One could hardly blame him for having second thoughts about loving her after that.

What if he sent her away?

Her anxiety level rose alarmingly, pumping adrenaline through her, making her feel wired and on edge. All she needed was for Steve to greet her with that impersonal, smiling glad-hand of his, the way he had done that fateful day last week, and she would lose it completely.

But Steve didn't say anything at all. Michelle found the tense silence even more unnerving than his de rigueur political smile and handshake. *Steve Saraceni couldn't summon a smile, however false?* It was unimaginable. He must really hate her, Michelle decided. She was too late, she'd said too much.

She had to get out of here before she fell apart in front of him. "I—I've c-come at a bad time," Michelle stammered, gulping back the sob that welled in her throat. "I'll just leave and—"

Steve crossed the office with the lithe speed of a pouncing cat. "No!" He took her hand, pulled her the whole way inside and closed the door. "You can't leave, Michelle."

He looked as worn and frazzled as she felt, light-years removed from the unruffled, urbane epitome of cool who'd greeted her here last week. Telltale signs of exhaustion enhanced his grim expression.

"I'll keep you here until I can make you understand the way I feel about you," Steve said passionately. "There has to be a way to convince you that I love you, Michelle. I'll find the right words if you'll just give me a chance."

He slid his hands up her arms and cupped her shoulders. Her nearness sent him reeling. He inhaled the light scent of her perfume, felt her warmth and softness under his hands. A shudder quaked his body. "Please, Michelle," he said hoarsely.

Joy surged through Michelle like an exploding rocket. Steve didn't hate her; he wasn't going to send her away. *He loved her!* And finally, she realized how much. "You've already proven it to me," she whispered, tears shining in her eyes.

She took a step forward, closing the small distance between them, and flung her arms around his neck. "Oh, Steve, I'm so sorry. I accused you of betraying me and my confidences, but I know that you didn't. You even tried to protect me. You could have defended yourself by telling me about Ed and Leigh, by saying that he was the one who gave you the inside information, but . . . but you didn't."

Steve's arms enfolded her in a tight, strong embrace. "I didn't have the heart to tell you what I knew about Dineen, Michelle. I knew how highly you regarded him, how much you admired the Dineens as the ideal family. I knew you would find out about his affair soon enough and that you'd be crushed to hear about it. I didn't want to be the one to hurt you with the news."

He drew back a little so he could gaze deeply into her eyes. "I've hurt you badly enough, Michelle. I was careless and got you pregnant and—"

"No!" she cried, laying her fingers against his lips to hush him. "Steve, you're wrong. I don't *blame* you for *getting* me pregnant. It takes two, remember? I'm equally responsible. And you know what? I'm thrilled about this baby. I want our child, Steve. And if you still want me to, I want to marry you and—"

He didn't give her time to finish. His mouth caught hers and held it, kissing her deeply, passionately, affirming the fact that they were together again. And that this time all the misunderstanding and mistrust was resolved and behind them.

When at last they reluctantly, breathlessly drew apart, Michelle gazed up at Steve, her china blue eyes swimming with tears that slowly trickled down her cheeks. He gently followed the track of one with his thumb. "Don't cry, honey," he said huskily. "I love you, Michelle. I thought it would never happen to me but when I met you I fell in love and I fell hard."

"Oh, Steve, I love you, too. And I should have trusted you, I should—"

"No recriminations, Michelle," he interrupted quietly. "I have too many of my own. I should have told you I loved you a long time ago. Then you wouldn't have felt insecure about my feelings for you, you would have known I wasn't just using you. And I most definitely should have taken you in my arms that day when you told me about the baby. I was so damn glad to see you, but I tried to act cool. I was still playing games then, looking to get the upper hand, but sweetheart, no more. I said all the wrong things when I should have told you how much I love you and want you and our child. Because it's true, Michelle. You're mine and we're going to be together forever."

"We—we won't end up like the Dineens," she whispered imploringly.

"Not a chance. I wouldn't throw away my life with you because some hot-to-trot political groupie throws herself at me. I've gotten all that out of my system, Michelle. I've grown up. Loving you doesn't tie me down, it's freed me from my selfishness and my, uh, frenetic restlessness."

"That's an interesting term for a social life that spanned four cities." Michelle looked up at him, her brows arched. "Your *life-style* before you met me was rather—peripatetic, to say the least."

"I'm giving up my *life-style* for a life, a real one." Steve laughed and hugged her, swinging her completely off the ground, turning around and around with her in his arms. Then he set her on her feet, letting her slide slowly down the length of his body, turning their release into an intimate, sensual caress.

"Come on, we're getting out of here." He took her hand and pulled her along with him. "We have to get rings and blood tests and a license."

"Can't we make love first?" Michelle asked breathily. "It's been so long and I've missed you so much, Steve."

"Sweetie, you don't have to ask twice."

Laughing, loving each other, they walked out of the office and into their future together.

Epilogue

Nine months later

"**I**t's a boy!" the doctor said exultantly, putting the wriggling, squalling newborn infant into the proud father's arms.

Steve was smiling broadly and his dark eyes were suspiciously moist as he showed Michelle their new son. She hardly had time to admire him, though, for she was otherwise occupied—giving birth to their daughter.

"A girl," proclaimed the doctor.

"She's beautiful!" breathed Steve. He handed the baby boy to Michelle so he could hold their daughter.

"A dark-haired girl and a blond boy," the nurse said with a happy sigh. "You have the perfect family."

"I have to agree with the nurse," Steve said later in the privacy of Michelle's hospital room. He was holding blue-eyed Jake while Michelle cuddled black-eyed Julie. "We are the perfect family." He leaned down to affectionately kiss his wife's forehead and she smiled up at him, love shining softly in her eyes.

Early in her pregnancy, tests had revealed the presence of twins and Steve couldn't have been more attentive and supportive to her throughout. Michelle knew he would be as devoted a father as he was a husband. Having committed himself to the role of family man, he thrust himself into it with his customary determination, vigor and zeal.

Because twins often come early and fast, the doctors had advised Michelle to stop working midway through her pregnancy, and though quitting her job would have been wrenching at one time, under the circumstances, she was relieved to leave Senator Dineen's office. Ed's affair with Leigh Wilson continued with an appalling lack of discretion and taste, leaving the rest of his staff angry and demoralized. One by one, resignations were handed in, and as word of Ed's scandalous behavior reached the folks in his district back home, point by point, his standing at the polls slowly sank. His re-election was seriously in doubt as a well-spoken, idealistic, happily-married contender had announced her intentions to run for the state senate seat.

With the twins needing her full time, Michelle decided to put her career on hold for a while, but she had a standing offer to work for Legislative Engineers Limited whenever she felt like venturing back into the Harrisburg scene.

"Oh, I almost forgot, this came for you in the mail today." Holding the baby in one arm, Steve handed Michelle a thick mailing bag. It was postmarked New York, New York.

"It's Ashlinn's manuscript!" Michelle grinned. "She promised she would send me a copy. She actually found a publisher and sold her book."

"She promised, hmm? Seems more like a threat to me." Steve helped her tear open the bag and remove the manuscript. "*Hooked!* What kind of a title is that?"

"It's about women who love men who don't love them," Michelle told him.

Steve set the manuscript aside. "You can't relate to that, Michelle. You love a man who loves you more than life itself." He gazed passionately into her eyes. "You know that, Michelle. Don't you?"

"Yes," she whispered, squeezing his hand. "I know, Steve."

*   *   *   *   *

NORA ROBERTS

Love has a language all its own, and for centuries, flowers have symbolized love's finest expression. Discover the language of flowers—and love—in this romantic collection of 48 favorite books by bestselling author Nora Roberts.

Starting in February 1992, two titles will be available each month at your favorite retail outlet.

In February, look for:

Irish Thoroughbred, Volume #1
The Law Is A Lady, Volume #2

Collect all 48 titles and become fluent in the Language of Love.

LOL 192

THE LANGUAGE of LOVE

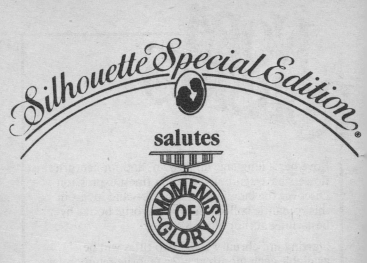

Silhouette Special Edition

salutes

MOMENTS OF GLORY

from Lindsay McKenna

In a country torn with conflict, in a time of bitter passions, these brave men and women wage a war against all odds... and a timeless battle for honor, for fleeting moments of glory, for the promise of enduring love.

February: RIDE THE TIGER (#721) Survivor Dany Villard is wise to the love-'em-and-leave-'em ways of war, but wounded hero Gib Ramsey swears she's captured his heart... forever.

March: ONE MAN'S WAR (#727) The war raging inside brash and bold Captain Pete Mallory threatens to destroy him, until Tess Ramsey's tender love guides him toward peace.

April: OFF LIMITS (#733) Soft-spoken Marine Jim McKenzie saved Alexandra Vance's life in Vietnam; now he needs her love to save his honor....

SEMG-1

Silhouette Romance

LONG, TALL TEXANS

DONAVAN
Diana Palmer

Diana Palmer's bestselling LONG, TALL TEXANS series continues with DONAVAN....

From the moment elegant Fay York walked into the bar on the wrong side of town, rugged Texan Donavan Langley knew she was trouble. But the lovely young innocent awoke a tenderness in him that he'd never known...and a desire to make her a proposal she couldn't refuse....

Don't miss DONAVAN by Diana Palmer, the ninth book in her LONG, TALL TEXANS series. Coming in January...only from Silhouette Romance. LTT192

Coming in February from

SILHOUETTE® *Desire*™

MAN OF
THE MONTH

THE BLACK SHEEP
by Laura Leone

Man of the Month Roe Hunter
wanted nothing to do with
free-spirited Gingie Potter.

Yet beneath her funky fashions
was a woman's heart—and body—
he couldn't ignore.

You met Gingie in
Silhouette Desire #507
A WILDER NAME
also by Laura Leone
Now she's back.

SDBL

YOU'VE ASKED FOR IT, YOU'VE GOT IT!

MAN OF THE MONTH: 1992

ONLY FROM

SILHOUETTE® *Desire*™

You just couldn't get enough of them, those sexy men from Silhouette Desire—twelve sinfully sexy, delightfully devilish heroes. Some will make you sweat, some will make you sigh . . . but every long, lean one of them will have you swooning. So here they are, men we couldn't resist bringing to you for one more year. . . .

A KNIGHT IN TARNISHED ARMOR
by Ann Major in January

THE BLACK SHEEP
by Laura Leone in February

THE CASE OF THE MESMERIZING BOSS
by Diana Palmer in March

DREAM MENDER
by Sheryl Woods in April

WHERE THERE IS LOVE
by Annette Broadrick in May

BEST MAN FOR THE JOB
by Dixie Browning in June

Don't let these men get away! *Man of the Month*, only in Silhouette Desire.